Kentucky D

Hearts are racing

Cousins Callee Dobson and Christina Mobbs are both dedicated to their patients. Callee to all the people at Churchill Downs, home of the Kentucky Derby, and Christina to her animals, including an equine contender for the derby who needs her care. These feisty Southern belles have both had their fair share of heartache, so it's easy for them to throw themselves into their work. Until trauma doc Langston Watts and Irish veterinarian Conor O'Brian arrive to give them a run for their money and put their hearts on the line...

Join Susan Carlisle's Kentucky Derby Medics as they buckle up for the greatest race of all—the final furlong to their happy-ever-afters.

Callee and Langston's story
Falling for the Trauma Doc
Available now

Christina and Conor's story
Coming soon

Dear Reader,

I enjoyed bringing this story to the page. I love horse racing and there's no better race than the Kentucky Derby. After a tour of the stable area, I soon learned, as with most things, there are many moving parts and people working behind the scenes to produce the big event.

This story is about some of those people. The ones who love and care for the horses while at the same time needing care themselves. That attention comes in the form of the bighearted Callee and the smart and supportive Langston.

I hope you enjoy reading their love story while they work at Churchill Downs.

Susan

Falling for the Trauma Doc

SUSAN CARLISLE

HARLEQUIN

MEDICAL
ROMANCE

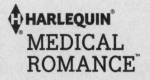

HARLEQUIN®
MEDICAL ROMANCE™

Recycling programs for this product may not exist in your area.

ISBN-13: 978-1-335-59544-7

Falling for the Trauma Doc

Harlequin Enterprises ULC
22 Adelaide St. West, 41st Floor
Toronto, Ontario M5H 4E3, Canada
www.Harlequin.com

Printed in U.S.A.

Susan Carlisle's love affair with books began when she made a bad grade in mathematics. Not allowed to watch TV until the grade had improved, she filled her time with books. Turning her love of reading into a love for writing romance, she pens hot medicals. She loves castles, traveling, afternoon tea, reading voraciously and hearing from her readers. Join her newsletter at susancarlisle.com.

Visit the Author Profile page
at Harlequin.com for more titles.

To Ava Grace

I love you dearly.

May May

CHAPTER ONE

CALLEE DOBSON STEPPED to the rail along the back turn of Churchill Downs Racetrack. She inhaled the damp, Louisville, Kentucky, morning air. The smell of dirt, hay and horses filled her nose. These she knew well from childhood. Leaning her arms along the railing, she watched the track in anticipation. The early morning run, the breeze as it was called, when the horses practiced, was the best part of the day. A girl could be taken off the horse farm, but the horse farm couldn't be taken out of the girl.

Having a veterinarian for a father, she loved the animals, but her place was with humans. Her father hadn't taken it well when she'd turned to human medicine just as she had been accepted to veterinary school. Years later he still wouldn't discuss her decision.

As the head of the medical clinic located in the stable area on the Churchill Downs grounds, she had the best of both worlds. Working in what was called the backside, she cared for the people who lived and worked there.

The thunder of hooves grew. She leaned forward. The sound became louder and louder.

Someone came to stand beside her. Callee glanced to her right. It was a man wearing a cowboy hat. She did a double take. Could a man be more out of place? She checked the track again. No horses yet. Covertly she studied the stranger. He wore a collared shirt in light blue with the cuffs rolled up a couple of times over his forearms. Jeans covered his long legs. He lifted a foot and braced it on the bottom rail. She blinked twice. His cowboy boots were dark brown. She grinned. Who was this guy? He must've gotten lost on his way west.

His vivid blue eyes that almost matched his shirt commanded her attention. "Mornin'."

The man's drawl reminded her of thick warm caramel flowing over a hotcake. For a second she came close to licking her lips. She did love a good Southern drawl on a man. Joe had had a drawl when he could speak. Her chest tightened. She didn't want to think about that.

The sound of huffing and puffing, and hooves hitting the ground filled the air. The horses and riders moved into the back stretch. The Thoroughbreds were spectacular in their beauty. She'd almost missed them by the time her attention returned to the track.

Watching the horses disappear in the mist, she looked at the man who reminded her of them, all sleek lines and rippling muscles. She had meteorically flipped over the fence with that thought.

Who was he anyway? She looked beyond him to see if he had come with a tour group but saw none.

"That was amazing," the man commented.

"It always is." She turned to go, due at the clinic in three minutes if it was to open on time.

"Do you watch often?" the man persisted.

She said over her shoulder, "Every morning."

"It must be tough on the jockey if one falls at that speed." He stepped up beside her.

"It can be." She needed to get away from this talkative tourist. "Have a good day." Sticking her hands in the back pockets of her jeans, she strolled over to the clinic building.

Located on the second street of the backside of the sprawling Churchill Downs complex, the small white building did not look like much from the outside, but she was proud of it. It had two front windows with a single glass door between them and the title above the door. A smaller building that shared a wall with the clinic held a school room for the jockeys and stable workers. It included a room with computers.

Callee unlocked the front door of the clinic and stepped inside. That area was just as immaculate as she had left it on Friday evening. She took great pride in everything looking just so. Flipping on the lights as she went, Callee headed toward the back where her office was located. She chuckled. It was more like a glorified closet, but it was her private domain. Carl, who handled the waiting area while she saw patients, knew that when her office door was closed not to bother her unless it involved a pouring-blood emergency.

At the sound of the front door opening and closing, she hollered, "Good morning, Carl. I'm back here. I haven't started coffee yet. Would you mind doing so?"

There was no response, but that wasn't unusual, so she continued around her desk and turned on her computer. A few minutes later the smell the coffee brewing reached her.

The thumping sound of boots against the concrete floor brought her brows together. Those footsteps didn't sound like Carl's. She stepped into the hall and jerked to a stop. The man who had been talking to her outside came toward her holding a mug with steam wafting from the top.

He no longer wore his hat. His thick, brown wavy hair looked as if he'd pushed it into some order using his fingers, but a lock still fell over his forehead. He smiled. A sexy one that made her stomach quiver. She took a moment to settle it.

"I brought you a cup of coffee." The Texas twang had her thinking of a warm summer night.

She took the offered cup. He had even gotten her mug correct. Her eyes narrowed. "I'm sorry, but who are you?"

He started back down the hall. "Do you mind if I get a cup before we talk?"

Who was this man? He certainly was bold. Her

stranger danger radar was going off. Surely Carl would be coming in soon. Callee followed the man down the hall. She had cared for a number of trainers and horse owners who had been arrogant, but this man might win the prize for being the most self-assured person she had met.

She put a note of firmness in her voice. "Can I help you?"

"No, I'll get it." His reply was causal, and unhurried.

Was he dense on purpose? She had been referring to why he was in her clinic. She waited behind him in the doorway while he poured his coffee. He liked it black. She wasn't surprised. He turned. She had to take a step back for him not to hit her with his cup.

"I'm Langston Watts. You should be expecting me."

Hadn't she read that name somewhere? She studied his face. Yeah, that email from the main office, the one from Dr. Bishop. She half read it before a patient came in. This guy was a doctor doing a study the track was participating in. "Oh, yes, I was."

"You had forgotten about me. That happens." The last two words had an unexpected note. Bitterness?

The man was wrong there. He wasn't someone she would have forgotten. If it wasn't for his hat and boots, then it would have been his drawl or his blue eyes. The man was a shining example of memorable.

Straightening to her five-foot-three-inch height, she didn't intend to let him intimidate her. "You're the doctor who wants to do head trauma evaluations on people who work with the horses."

"Yep, there it is, that's me. Your boss has agreed to let Valtech, the company I work with, do research on head injuries here. To help us develop more protective headgear."

"That sounds like something useful, but you do know we're coming up on the busiest week of the year around here. There'll be all kinds of people and horses coming and going." She twisted her cup between her hands.

"I realize Derby Week is in a few weeks. That's what makes it such a good time to do my research, because there's so many jockeys and trainers and people who work in the stalls here to study." He shrugged a shoulder. "What better time to get as much information as I can?"

She gave him a pointed look. "Just remember patient care comes first here."

He looked around the waiting area with its handful of chairs. "I'm also here to help with that as needed. I understood the deal with Churchill Downs was I'd also assist you."

She studied him a moment with a skeptical look. What kind of care could a researcher offer? "How much emergency care work have you done?"

"Quite a bit. I'm a trauma physician. I assure you I can handle whatever comes." He took a seat in one of the beat-up plastic chairs and rested his ankle over his knee.

"I certainly hope so." She looked at the door when it opened.

Carl entered. "Hey, boss." He gave Langston a questioning look.

Langston stood and extended his hand. "Dr. Langston Watts. But you can call me Langston."

"Carl." Callee hesitated a moment than said, "Langston is here to do a study. He'll also be helping us with patients as needed."

Carl nodded. "Great. We can use the help. Especially around the Derby."

Langston looked at her. "And may I call you Callee?"

She'd not even had a chance to introduce herself, but he apparently had done his homework. "Sure. We're not formal around here."

"That's good to hear." He took a sip of his coffee and looked at her. "How about showing me around?"

She and Carl looked at each other, smiled. "You've pretty much seen it all, but I'll give you the grand tour if you want."

"I want."

Callee had no doubt he hadn't meant that to sound like an innuendo, but her mind had gone there. What was this reaction she had to him?

Since her college boyfriend, she remained cautious and in control about any interest she had in a man. She didn't deserve to have these feelings, yet they were springing up. Why this guy and why now?

At the sound of the clinic door opening, she turned. One of her favorite exercise riders hurried in holding a wrapped hand with blood seeping through his fingers. She rushed to him. "What happened, Jose?"

"The new horse in Barn Seven caught me against the wall while I was cleaning his hoof." He spoke in heavily accented English, and Spanish.

That was her weakness at work. Her Spanish was poor. She'd been trying to improve it by using an online program but wasn't making much progress. She needed to ask medical questions. Not where the nearest diner was located.

Langston spoke rapidly in Spanish to Jose.

She was jealous of his ability having only caught a few words. "Come back to an exam room. Take a seat in the chair."

Jose did as she requested. "I'm going to give this a look. We'll need to make sure it isn't broken."

Langston stood close enough she could feel his body heat.

She slowly unwrapped the rag from Jose's hand. He winced. "I'm being as gentle as I can be."

"I know, Ms. Callee."

She studied the angry, swollen hand already

turning blue and purple. He would need stitches and an X-ray.

"You have an X-ray machine?" Langston asked.

"I do."

"Good." Langston shifted as if trying to get a better look.

Not that she needed his approval, but at least after the embarrassing moments over the coffee she felt redeemed. "Jose, we're gonna need to X-ray your hand."

"I not go to hospital. Work." The smaller man looked at her, panic filling his eyes.

Langston spoke to him in Spanish faster than she could follow. Jose nodded.

"I told him that we'd take some pictures to see if it was broken before we decided if he needed to go to the hospital or not." Langston stepped away from her and continued in English. "If we need to send you to the hospital, we'll still get a note for you to give your boss."

Once again, an unsure look came over Jose's face.

Langston repeated what he'd said in Spanish. Jose nodded.

She touched Jose's arm and pointed to the door. She led the way down the hall to a room across from her office. An old but still reliable X-ray machine stood there. She carefully put a vest over Jose's hand and then set it on his shoulders. Lifting his hand to the table of the machine, she placed the palm down. "Stay right like that and stay still."

Langston stepped out into the hall, and she joined him. Callee clicked a switch and there was a buzz.

"All done," she announced as she reentered the room.

Langston helped Jose off with the vest while she reviewed the X-ray on a screen.

Carl came to the door.

"Carl, please take Jose back to the exam room and give him a couple of over-the-counter painkillers."

To Jose she said, "I'll see you in a minute."

Jose nodded.

She turned back to the X-ray.

Langston came to stand behind her. "Mind if I look too?"

Even if she did, he had already started studying the picture. She didn't see any broken bones, zooming in on each carpal and metacarpal finding nothing that looked damaged. She continued to search for a dark line indicating a fracture. The only sound in the room was that of them breathing. It was too intimate. He had pushed into her personal space. They didn't even know each other. She gave him a slight elbow to the middle. A torso that felt hard and fit. He grunted.

"Sorry. I didn't know you were so close." She stepped away from him.

His gaze met hers. A slight lift to one corner of his mouth implied he didn't believe her.

"Don't you think he needs an orthopedic doctor to have a look?"

She pursed her lips. "He won't go. If he doesn't work, he doesn't get paid. He has a family he sends money to. I'll send this X-ray over to an orthopedic guy who'll look at it. If he sees any problems, I'll talk to the trainer Jose works for and have him insist he go see the doctor."

Langston nodded. "Nice system, Callee. I bet your husband does all sorts of things he doesn't want to do but ends up glad to do it."

"I don't have a husband, and you make it sound like I'm a manipulating woman. I'm not flattered."

He raised a hand in defense. "Hey, I didn't mean to insult you."

"I don't think you meant to flatter me either." She didn't hide the bitter taste in her voice.

He gave her a direct look. "No, I'm impressed."

She narrowed her eyes and clicked off the screen. Jose was waiting. "Surprisingly, it all looks really good."

"I agree."

Callee started toward the door. "I do appreciate the second opinion." She headed straight to Jose's exam room. "Jose, it doesn't look like you've broken anything. I'm going to clean and wrap your hand. No work."

"I must work. I have stalls to clean." Jose looked almost frantic.

"That's not going to happen for you today. We'll see about tomorrow. For today you'll have to get someone else to do it for you. If you need me to write a note, just let me know. I don't think it'll take too much for Ron to see you can't hold a pitch-fork. Do you understand?"

The man slowly nodded.

"Now let's get your hand cleaned up and ban-daged." Carl had already laid out a bottle of saline and a pan. There was roll of gaze and a tan stretch bandage waiting as well.

Langston stood across the small room watch-ing as she poured the saline over Jose's hand and looked at it closely. "You're lucky not to need any stitches," Callee commented.

Holding Jose's hand carefully, she wrapped the gauze around it, being sure to cover any area with open skin. Over that she applied the stretch ban-dage. To help with the aching, she put an ice pack on the bandaged wound for twenty minutes.

"Keeping your hand above your heart will also help with the throbbing. I'll give you something for pain as well."

Jose nodded.

"Let me know if you have any problems. Come back tomorrow. I'll call you if the orthopedic doc-tor thinks he needs to see you. I'll get you an ice pack to take with you." She left the room. As she returned, she heard Langston speaking Spanish. Even in a different language his voice sounded nice. She could make out enough to know they were talking about being hit in the head.

Soon she sent Jose on his way.

As soon as the man left, she looked at Langston. "Still want that quick tour? Then again, you've already seen most of the place. Afterward we'll go to my office and talk about this study you're doing and how I can help."

Before they had time to walk down the hall another patient entered.

During the morning, Langston had been surprised at how busy the clinic could be. A couple of times Callee had allowed him to do the initial assessment, but she'd been in to see the patient. He might be the physician, but this was her clinic. He wasn't used to working under someone else's direction. His inability to do so had made it difficult in a couple of places he had worked. He might have been right, yet the head of the department didn't like having that pointed out. Langston soon had to move on. That was one thing about his current job—he only took orders from himself.

By the time lunchtime came around, he and Callee had seen sniffles, a rash, and any number of regular everyday aches and pains. Langston had been impressed. Callee had given each one the same amount of attention regardless of how simple their complaint might have been. She treated them all as if they were her friends. She knew each by name and if she didn't, she made sure she introduced herself and practiced using their name. Callee was so personable. He'd seen nothing like it in his work.

He'd gotten the impression she wasn't that pleased to have him around. He couldn't decide if it was because he was encroaching on her territory or because she didn't care for him, or he made her nervous. Whatever it was, he would figure it out. He would be at Churchill Downs six weeks and wanted them to be pleasant. He had a job to do, an important one, then he would move on.

Before agreeing to do head trauma research, he'd worked in a large hospital in the neurological unit with a world-renowned staff. The problem was the head of the department believed there was only one way to care for a particular patient. He and Langston had disagreed, vehemently. Working in the department had become so difficult that Langston had snatched up the opportunity to work with Valtech, the makers of Head Armor. Yet leaving the hospital had taken him away from the personal side of medicine. Working at the clinic that morning he'd found he'd missed it.

"You ready for lunch?" Callee asked after the latest patient went out the door.

"I could eat." His stomach growled. There

hadn't been time for even a full cup of coffee that morning.

"Then I'll take you to the best restaurant in town. Where we are going has the best breakfast in Louisville. And the burgers aren't bad. Let me get my money." She started toward her office.

"I'll get your meal for letting me work with you." Langston headed for the front door.

"I can't let you do that." Something about letting him pay felt like a date.

"Sure you can. You can pay the next time. Are we going far? Should I drive?"

"Nope. It's just three barns away." She pushed the door open.

"Really? Three barns, huh."

He sounded amazed by the idea of those directions. "Yep, it's just across the street from the backside so it's where everybody around here eats, and a number of those who have read about it make a point to come in."

Langston pursed his lips. "Interesting. I'm looking forward to the place already."

She called over her shoulder to Carl. "We're going over to the Brown Derby for lunch. You want me to bring you back something?"

"I'll go over when you get back. Maybe it'll have calmed down for the day."

"Okay."

She led the way around the corner of the building and down the road through the barns, waving at a few people as she went.

Langston watched, amazed. "You feel at home here, don't you?"

"Yep. I found where I belong. Despite not having anything major after Jose's hand, we had a busier than normal morning. I appreciate your help. You didn't have to, you know."

"I didn't mind. It was good to see patients again." He hadn't said anything, but he was also anxious to get started on his research.

"You haven't been doing that?" She looked at him in disbelief.

He worked to match his long stride to her shorter ones. "No. Recently I've mostly been reviewing charts."

Callee tsked. "I like paper pushing the least."

"Do you ever handle cases of head injuries involving the horses and riders?" He needed some good solid cases to look into.

"Sure, but not as often as you would think. I act as first responder on those, but the rider is always taken to the hospital. At the minimum put under concussion procedures."

"Gotcha." He looked down the street they crossed to see more barns beyond. At each end of the barns was another street. The barns were painted the same color with occasional colored accents. Someone could easily get lost because every building looked so much like the others.

"Why don't you explain to me more about why you're here so maybe I can help you." Callee stopped to let a truck pulling a horse trailer go by.

"They didn't tell you anything about what I'm doing?"

"The front office isn't known for being clear. They just told me to expect you, which I managed not to do." She grinned.

"I'm studying head traumas over the next six weeks. I also agreed to help out in the clinic since the population on the backside will grow leading up to the Derby."

"How do you plan to do this study?" She waved to a man at the other end of a barn.

"I'll be looking through your files on patients who have come in with head injuries and reviewing them. If they are still working here, I'd like to interview them. I would also be reviewing and interviewing any patients with issues while I'm here. I'd also like to interview all your patients over the next few weeks to see if any of them have experienced head injuries in the past. When patients come in, I want to talk to them about any head injuries they may have experienced in the past, be it a fall from a hayloft or involving a horse."

"I get the obvious connection between the horseracing industry and technology."

"There are quite a number of head injuries, or opportunities for them in horse racing. I plan to do cognitive tests. I understand that everyone is

required to have a yearly checkup or present a report that they have had one. When they come in,
I'd like to do additional studies, with their permission, of course."

Their feet crunched on the gravel as they continued down the street.

She gave him a doubtful look. "You think your
gonna see everyone working here in six weeks?
That's pretty ambitious."

He would try. Failure wasn't a word in his vocabulary. Despite doing so where Emily had been
concerned. But he had no intention of letting that
happen again. Because he'd never let himself be
in a position to care like that. That's why he was
known for being good at his job. He focused on it.
"Maybe not everyone but as many as I can."

"Have you always done research?"

"No, like I said, my background is in emergency
trauma."

"Wow, research and working at my small clinic
don't sound like they would be high adrenaline
enough for you. What got you out of trauma?"

"I still keep my hand in at the trauma units even
when I travel. I do visiting doctor work as well."

"Why head trauma?"

He shrugged. "I slowly became interested in
head trauma as I worked with car accident victims
and children who had bike accidents and falls. I
seemed to gravitate to those cases. I'd be the one
called on to care for those patients.

"One particular patient, a cute white-blond little girl came in with a head injury that could have been prevented if the helmet hadn't cracked. I said to myself, *This has to stop*. That's when I agreed to do research on finding a better product to protect children like that little girl. I wanted to make a lasting difference. Not just fix them up to go out there and do it again."

She nodded. Her eyes having turned serious. "What can do I do to help you?"

They came to another cross street. A truck headed their way. He grabbed her elbow to stop her. Her face turned rebellious. He let go. What had gotten into him? He wasn't usually so overprotective. The truck passed in a small cloud of gray dust.

"I need access to the records and for you to encourage your past and present patients to talk to me. Based on what I've seen so far you know everyone."

"Sounds simple enough. I'll do what I can. It may be tough. This is a close-knit world, and they're suspicious of others."

Langston wouldn't expect less than what he needed. More than one person had told him he was an overachiever. He'd graduated from high school a year earlier than he should have with glowing grades. Medical college fed his hunger for knowledge, and he'd breezed through it. Now he had a number of degrees, had traveled all over the world presenting papers on his work and was considered an authority in the field of head trauma. The only thing he had been accused of was not having a personal life. That, he didn't care anything about having. Hurt lay there.

At one time he had been involved with a girl. He and Emily had planned a life together. He would go to the Peace Corps for two years so he could get Prairie, Texas, the small town they live in, purged from his system. Then he'd return and go to medical school. When Emily finished college, they'd get married. With his fellowship completed he'd start his practice in Dallas, not in a small town where nothing happened.

Instead, he had returned from overseas to learn Emily and his best friend, Mark, had become involved while he was gone. He and Mark had been inseparable when they were kids. Then it had been Langston and Emily as teens. Often Mark joined them. He had even been Langston's college roommate.

Devastated and heartbroken, Langston put all his energy and emotion into his work. He promised himself he'd never open his heart again. To a woman or to a best friend. He'd not only lost his girlfriend but a major part of his life with the loss of Mark. That had been as painful as breaking up with Emily had been.

His entire focus at this point in his life was to

gather enough data to improve the quality of helmets in order to save lives.

He and Callee continued walking.

"It looks like the backside is set up on a grid system?"

"Yes. The end of each barn is the corner of a street. They run in front and behind the barns with the exception of a couple of streets where there are grassy areas. The roads have street names, but most people go by the barns' names. Those names are the trainers who lease them."

They came to a main road that was the back boundary of the lot. Callee looked in both directions before crossing. "What do you know about the people who work around a racetrack?"

"I haven't been around horses much. Or racetracks for that matter." Why did he feel a twinge of guilt about that?

She stopped and looked him up and down. "I thought you were a cowboy."

He felt the need to straighten his shoulders. "I'm a Texan who likes hats and boots. That doesn't mean I was raised on a ranch. Sorry to disappoint you."

She chuckled. "If you don't care for horses, you've come to the wrong place."

This small woman wasn't going to intimidate him. "Then I'll need you to help me. I'm a quick learner. I do know how to care for people."

"What exactly do you want to know about people who work with horses?"

"Everything." He did. The more he knew the better the chance of getting the information he needed.

"I don't know if I can give you that, but I can give you some general info." She waved a hand around. "As you know, this is considered the backside. The barns are rented out by trainers. Some barns are held in reserve for the horses that come in for special races."

"Like the Derby."

"Yep." She warmed to her subject.

"If the trainers don't have enough horses for a full barn, they rent stalls out. It's a transit lifestyle for jockeys, trainers and their staff along with the horses."

He liked that idea. It was much like his lifestyle. "You don't mind working where everyone is coming and going?"

"Not really. I just look forward to their return. On the way back I'll show you some points of interest." She grinned. Callee stopped at another cross street and pointed to the right. "See that three-story brick building? That's the workers' dormitory. Some live here year-round. Many need to be close to the horses."

"I had no idea."

"A number of these workers come from all around the world. They're great with horses, but they're not all familiar with the English language. As you saw this morning, it can make it interesting at the clinic."

Spanish came easy to him. "Do you have interpreters?"

A sad look appeared on her face. "Sometimes I can find one. Other times it's more about sign language. Some use translation apps. That can make it interesting."

"I'm sure it does. What time of the day do things get started each morning? I need to plan for my interviews."

"Just before daylight. The breeze is finished early morning before the heat of the day. Then there is cooling down, washing, grooming and feeding of the horses. While that's going on others are cleaning out the stalls. By midday things are settling down." She chuckled. "We're on horse schedule around here."

"Makes sense." He'd adjust. After all, he had done that more than once in his life.

"Now things are different during the month of April. Leading up to the Derby, things get crazier by the day here. By the time Derby Week arrives, we're busy all the time."

"That's a big deal around here." He at least had heard of the Kentucky Derby but never had any real interest in it.

"The biggest. I forgot." She turned in the opposite direction. "Over there's our full-time veterinary clinic." She pointed to the large single-story building. "It stays busy all the time. The horses are constantly checked for various different reasons, including being drug tested."

"Do you handle blood testing for the jockeys?"

"There's a special procedure for them on race weeks, and a special group sometimes uses the clinic for gathering tests. I couldn't handle it all myself. And they are very particular."

He couldn't help but be in awe. The more he knew the more he didn't know. "This really is a world unto itself."

"Yep, a pretty special one."

Langston could already tell that not only was the place special, but Callee was as well.

CHAPTER TWO

CALLEE ENTERED THE older building with a low ceiling, which had apparently been around for a long time. She glanced over her shoulder to see Langston duck to enter, and grinned. He was a tall one. The door closed behind them, leaving the pair in dim light.

"This reminds me of a good Texas bar." He stood in the doorway looking around.

Square wooden tables and chairs were filled with people in work shirts, jeans and boots. The busy room was noisy, but not deafening.

Callee searched for a table. "Looks like we're at the bar today." She took a seat next to a large man with dirt and dust covering his clothes. "Move over, Macomb. Let me have a seat."

The man looked over his shoulder. "Hell, Callee, you could sit in my pocket."

Callee grinned. "The problem is I want to sit in this chair not your pocket."

She dipped her shoulder, giving him a nudge, and climbed on the stool.

Langston took the empty seat beside her. His knees brushed her from hip to knee, sending an electric current through her. She glanced at him.

She certainly wasn't his type. A leggy woman, wearing makeup, nails done and fashionably dressed came to mind. Not the kind who had their hair pulled back, wore T-shirts, jeans and work boots. Like her. Nope she wasn't his type at all.

A man wearing a white apron tied around his waist asked Callee from the other side of the bar, "Hey, what're you having today?"

"A burger and fries," she called without looking at the menu.

The man looked at Langston.

"I'll have the same."

"And two sodas, Fred." Callee flashed a smile. He nodded and left.

"Hey, Callee, you going to make the game next Wednesday night?" Rick asked as he strolled by.

"Yeah, I'll be there."

"See you then." Rick waved a hand.

"What's that all about?" Langston asked.

She pushed the napkin holder back, making room in front of her. "We have a monthly poker game next door to the clinic at the community center."

"You're very much a part of the family around here."

He said that with an easiness she wouldn't have thought he felt. Something about Langston made her think of stable, safe and sure. Not fly-by-night. "I try to be. For all the reasons I told you earlier,

I work to have people trust me. It makes my job easier."

"I've never stayed in one place long enough to have a group to play poker with."

"While you're here you can join us." She picked up the glass Fred had just set in front of her.

Langston looked at her. Really looked at her as if he saw her. "Thanks. I just might do that. You like working here, don't you?"

She smiled. "Yeah. I do."

"How long have you been here?"

Why so much interest in her? "A couple of years."

Their burgers in a basket with fries were placed in front of them.

"What made you decide to do this type of work?"

Callee hoped he didn't notice the sadness filling her eyes before she blinked. She had no intention of telling him that awful story.

"I did my internship while working on getting my physician assistant degree here. The doctor I worked with retired, and I applied for the job. At that time, I really needed to be here." Callee had almost said too much. She ate her burger.

Half an hour later, Langston let the screen door close behind them on their way out of the restaurant. He rubbed his middle. "I have to say that was one of the best burgers I've ever eaten."

"I thought you might like it." She headed across the road. "You should try the breakfast sometime."

"I'll keep that in mind." He walked beside her on the way back to the clinic. She didn't reach his shoulder.

"Hey, Callee." Someone called her name.

Callee looked between the barns. She raised her hand to wave. "Hi, Gina." She looked at Langston. "I need to check on some stitches I put in a few days ago."

He stopped walking. "House call?"

She grinned. "More like a barn call."

"I thought those went the way of the dodo bird." Langston kicked at a rock.

She headed across the grassy area toward Gina, who sprayed water over a horse. "Not when it's your best friend you're checking on."

"Makes sense."

She looked at him. "Can you find your way to the clinic?"

"No problem."

"See you in a few then." She watched those long legs carry him down the road. He was almost as good-looking from behind as he was from the front. She started walking toward Gina.

Callee should have introduced Langston to Gina, but she needed a few minutes away from him. He was too much for her nervous system, and he'd only been there a few hours. Approaching Gina, Callee asked, "How's your hand doing?"

Gina held it up. It was inside a plastic glove.

"Smart idea. You don't need to get it infected."

She and Gina had met just after Callee had come to work at the Downs. They became friends immediately. Gina was on her way to becoming a great trainer. Currently she worked as a groom.

Gina looked beyond Callee to where Langston had just been. "Who was that tall drink of water you were with?"

"New doctor. He's here doing research."

"He could do research on me." Gina wiggled her brows. "Or maybe on you."

"Don't start." Gina knew her secrets. Knew why Callee couldn't go past being a friend with a man. Why she couldn't trust herself to care.

"Callee, you need to give guys a chance. What happened to you with Joe was a fluke. You need to let yourself off the hook."

"I know. I've moved on. I'm working here and have a good life."

Gina rolled her eyes. "Yeah. When was your last date?"

"It has been a while." Callee waved the comment away. "Instead of worrying about my love life you need to be worrying about yours."

"It's more fun to tease you about yours. If you don't want him, can I have him?"

That idea didn't appeal to Callee. "Enough about Langston. Again, how's your hand doing?"

"His name is Langston. I like that. Very sexy."

"Gina, the hand." Callee couldn't help but smile.

"I'm taking care of it." Gina removed the glove and showed Callee. "Someone made me get a tetanus shot. I don't wanna have to do that again."

Callee took Gina's hand, checking for redness or an opening in the incision. "Looks good. Don't forget to stop by and have those stitches out day after tomorrow."

"Can I meet the new guy then?" Gina's eyes twinkled.

Callee laughed. "If we aren't too busy."

"You sure you don't want to keep him to yourself?"

"I'm sure." What would she do if she did have Langston? Callee wouldn't deserve him. She shouldn't be happy after what she let happen to Joe. He was gone and it was all her fault. Callee shook her head. "You're man crazy. See you later."

"Why don't you invite him to poker this month? I could really get to know him."

"I already have." Maybe she should have given that more thought. Callee wasn't sure she wanted Langston to encroach on her private time since he already had so much of her work time. Why it would matter she had no idea. By his own admission he came and went. If she did become interested in a man, it would be one who had the potential to settle down and eventually have a family. That wasn't Langston.

But would it be so bad to flirt with him while

he was in town? She harrumphed. What did she know about flirting anymore? It had been a long time since she'd done that.

Twenty minutes later she entered the clinic to find Carl and Langston laughing over something. Both of them looked guilty and quickly hushed.

She looked at Langston. "We should be pretty quiet this afternoon. I'll show you how to access the files."

Langston brought in his legs and stood. "Sounds good."

They walked to her office. Callee put in her passwords. "I saw in the email from the front office that you had clearance to be in the files for head injuries only."

"Yeah." He came to stand beside her.

He had a way of making her too aware of him. Did he mean to? She shook her head. They didn't even know each other. "I have to follow the laws here as well."

"Understood."

The screen opened. "The files you should need are right here. Let me know if you need some help. I'll leave you with it." She bumped him on her way to the door. An electric pulse shot through her.

"Sorry." He shifted out from behind the desk, giving her space to pass.

"I don't know how comfortable you're going to be in here. But it's the best I can do."

Her rolling chair creaked under his weight when

he sat. "Don't worry. I'll manage. If you get busy, call me."

"I appreciate it." She saw most of her patients in the mornings and spent the afternoons catching up on paperwork and making phone calls. She planned to share Carl's desk for a while. Earlier in the day she'd heard back from the orthopedist about Jose's hand, which wasn't broken. She needed to call him. If she couldn't get him on the phone, she would go to the barn where he worked and look for him.

By the time Callee walked back from seeing Jose, it was time to close the clinic for the day. She hadn't seen Langston in hours. She went to her office to find him studying the screen with a pen in his hand and a pad on the desk beside him. "Sorry to bother you but it's time to close up for the day."

Langston's head popped up. He leaned back in the chair, put his hands behind his head and stretched. His shirt tightened across his broad chest. She couldn't stop herself from looking.

"I'm sorry. I get so engrossed in this type of stuff I forget what time it is."

"That's what happens when you love what you do." She couldn't help but admire his work ethic.

His look softened. "I'm glad you understand. Quite a few people don't. I've dated women who thought I got a little obsessive."

"We all get obsessive about what we love."

He stood. "It's just nice to meet someone who understands. Let me get my stuff together and I'm on my way out."

A few minutes later they parted company. She watched him walk to a large late model red pickup truck. For a moment she wondered how he spent his evenings. He didn't seem like the kind of person who stayed at home reading a book. Did he go to a hospital to help out or volunteer in a night clinic?

Langston had been busy in Callee's office going through medical files for the last five days. Each day started the same. He met Callee at the track to watch the morning run, then they walked to the clinic.

She saw patients while he worked in her office. A few times she had asked for his help with a patient. He had joined her when Jose had come in to have his hand reexamined. When her friend Gina had stopped by to have her stitches removed, Callee had brought her back to meet him. Langston quickly decide he liked her.

In the afternoon Callee would work up front, and at five she closed the clinic. They'd stroll to their vehicles and say goodbye.

Heaven help him, he was turning into his parents. Living the same old pattern over and over. He shook his head and focused on the screen in front of him. There were only a few more weeks before he would be moving on. Yet something about this place had lulled him into a rut. The sad thing was he didn't seem to mind.

"Langston—" Callee's head popped inside the office "—bring your bag. I need your help."

He shoved out of his chair. "It's in the truck. What's up?"

"I'm needed at one of the barns." She'd already started up the hall. "A groom was kicked and they're afraid to move him. An ambulance is on the way."

Langston hurried after her, going out the front door. He loped to his truck, grabbed his bag. She pulled up in a golf cart. He climbed in. Callee floored the gas.

"How far?"

"Two barns down and one over." He held on as the wheels threw rocks as they went. Callee made a wild turn that almost threw him out of the vehicle. Halfway along the length of the barn she pulled to a jarring stop. People stood outside a stall of a well-kept barn with red doors and ferns hanging along the porch area. A horse stood outside a stall on its lead held by a young woman.

"Move back and let us through," Callee stated with the authority of a seven-foot giant.

The group parted, allowing himself and Callee through. They continued until they reached a concrete floor covered in sawdust. A young Hispanic man lay on the floor with two other men squatting beside him.

Callee didn't hesitate to go down on her knees next to the injured man. "What's your name?"

Langston watched from above.

"Carlos." The word came out as a gurgle. His face twisted with the effort to speak.

"Carlos, can you tell me where it hurts?"

The man lay a hand over his right side.

"Okay, I'm going to look for broken bones. Dr. Watts here," she said, nodding toward Langston, "is going to check you out too."

Carlos's eyelids drooped.

She lightly shook the man's shoulder. "Carlos, we need you to stay wake. I know it hurts, but I need to know where the pain is."

While Langston did vitals, she moved her hands over Carlos's chest. He moaned when she touched his right side. "He has broken ribs."

"Heart rate one-sixty over ninety. BP one-twenty over eighty-seven. Pulse one-forty. Respiration eighty. Labored breathing. He's going into shock." Without another thought, Langston removed his shirt and placed it over the man's chest for warmth. Jerking a horse blanket down off a hanger, he rolled it up and put it under his Carlos' feet to make them higher than his heart.

Callee continued to search for additional injuries.

Langston listened to Carlos's chest. Hearing a

sucking of air he said, "He has a punctured lung as well."

Callee took Carlos's hand and studied his nail beds.

Even in the filtered light of the stall's interior, Langston could tell they were a dusky blue.

Langston handed Callee the stethoscope. She listened to Carlos's lungs. "Agreed."

The sound of the ambulance coming, then the abrupt quiet after they turned off the siren said they were close.

"Thank goodness. He needs oxygen ASAP. The ambulance isn't far away. They turn the siren off because it will upset the horses."

Langston nodded. "Makes sense."

Minutes later the emergency medical technicians entered the stall with a stretcher. Callee quickly and succinctly gave a report to the EMTs.

Langston helped lift Carlos onto the stretcher. In no time the injured man and the ambulance had left. He leaned against the wooden wall. "How often is it like this?"

"Seems like more often now that you are around." She picked up his shirt from the floor, studying him. "Very heroic, Dr. Watts."

He grinned. She seemed to like what she saw. "I try." He reached out his hand. "Mind if I get my shirt back."

A sweet pink blush came to Callee's cheeks. She thrust the garment at him. "Uh…no, not at all."

Langston shrugged into his now dirty shirt and buttoned it. He packed his medical bag then stepped out into the bright sunshine behind Callee. A self-satisfied smile covered his lips. Callee could be rattled after all. He looked forward to doing it again sometime.

Callee berated herself for staring at Langston. She shouldn't have been doing that. After all, she was a professional. In her defense there had been a lot to admire. Broad shoulders with defined muscles, with a dusting of hair that included a line leading to a trim waist. It was all well worth viewing. She just wished she hadn't been caught doing so.

Langston grabbed her arm as she started to climb behind the wheel of the golf cart. "Oh, no. I'm driving. I'm not taking another *Mr. Toad's Wild Ride* back to the clinic."

"But—

"There is no but. Climb in or walk. I'm commandeering your ride."

She let him have his way and took the passenger seat. "I'm only agreeing because I appreciated your help back there."

"Not a problem." Langston made the turn at the end of the barn smoothly.

Callee cocked her ear. Even over the noise of the wheels of the cart she knew that sound. Fear shot through her. "Stop!"

"What's wrong?" Langston pressed on the brakes, jerking them to a skidding stop.

"That horse is wheezing." Her heart raced. She jumped off the golf cart. "They need to get the horse out of here."

She hurried to the man standing by the horse trailer. "Put him back in the trailer now."

"I was told to wait here." The groom looked perplexed about what his actions should be.

She kept her voice low and firm. "The horse has the flu. Get your trainer now."

The groom's eyes widened. He handed the lead off to another groom standing nearby. He nodded and shot off like he was being chased by a wild stallion.

To the man now holding the horse she said, "Don't go any farther than right here." She pointed to the spot at the end of the trailer. "Do not put that horse in the barn. Understood? I'm calling the vet right now."

"What's wrong?" Langston came to stand beside her with a confused look on his face.

"Horse flu. It's highly contiguous. It could shut down the entire Derby. This horse must be quarantined right now."

A man stalked toward her, his face ruby with anger. Behind him hurried the first groom. "What's going on here?" the man demanded, stepping into her personal space, glaring down his nose at her. "You have no business handling my horse."

Langston moved to where he could get between Callee and the man if needed.

She had to admit she liked having his support. Callee said in a low even voice, "This horse has the flu."

The trainer took a step back, his face turned ashen. "What?"

"I'm going to have to ask you to reload him. Now."

"You have no authority," the man spat, moving toward her again.

"Stay right there," Langston growled.

Callee could handle herself, but it was nice to know she had someone on her side. "No. But I'm calling the vet, who does."

"Get him in the trailer," the trainer barked at the groom.

Callee stepped across the road out of the way. Langston joined her. She watched as the men worked to get the horse back in the trailer. She pulled her phone out and pushed in the number for the Derby Veterinarian Clinic. She raised her voice an octave so it would carry to the men working with the horse. "May I speak to Dr. Dillard?"

The trainer glared at her. Callee raised her chin. She quickly relayed her information.

Finished with her call, she started toward the trainer. Langston didn't miss a step she made. Staying out of reach of the man she said, "Dr. Dillard is expecting you at the clinic."

The trainer turned his back to her.

She and Langston waited until the truck and trailer had turned the corner into the road leading to the vet clinic before she headed back to the golf cart.

"What's the urgency?" Langston asked as he climbed into the cart.

"If the horse comes into contact with any other horses, they will all be quarantined. As I said, horse flu is highly contagious. In fact, the dirt, all the sawdust where this horse stood must be removed and burned. All buckets must be sterilized." Callee took her place in the cart.

Langston started the vehicle. "What you did back there was impressive and crazy at the same time. Where did you learn to recognize horse flu? Working around here?"

"No, my father is a veterinarian. I used to go to work with him all the time."

Langston started down the road. "Really. I'm surprised you didn't become a veterinarian."

"It wasn't from him not wanting me to." If he had his way, she would be a veterinarian. She hated she had disappointed him.

"You make it sound like he wasn't happy when you didn't become a vet."

Langston was perceptive. She must be careful, or he would know all her secrets. "He wasn't. He's still disappointed."

"But you would like to make him happy." The statement held no criticism.

"Yeah. He's my hero. From the time I was a small kid I followed him around. If I wasn't in school, then I was in a barn caring for an animal or on a call with Dad. In college I had every intention of going to vet school."

Langston looked at her. "So why didn't you?"

"Because I thought I could make a more important difference if I did human medicine." Now they were getting into a territory she didn't like to share.

"Something significant must have happened to make you change your mind."

Her fingers tightened on the support to the top of the golf cart. Langston was digging where she didn't want him to. "Yeah. It did."

"Will you tell me about it?"

Callee looked around at the barns, the horse with its head out of the stall, the exercise boy washing a horse nearby. Could she tell the story? How she had failed someone she cared about. What would Langston think of her then?

He didn't say anything and neither did she for a few seconds.

She drew in a breath. "I was in my last year of college. My boyfriend and I were out celebrating my acceptance into vet school with some friends. We rarely went out to have a good time because we studied so much. Joe was planning to be a doctor."

Langston's body tensed as if preparing for what would come next.

"He drank far too much before I knew it. I was so caught up in talking and having a good time myself to be aware of what he had. He wasn't used to it so a little went a long way. I didn't realize how affected he was until Joe staggered to the car. I wouldn't let him drive. He got mad and jerked the keys out of my hand and drove off. I ran back and found a friend who would help me follow Joe. We found him." She went quiet for a moment. "Joe had crashed into a tree. There wasn't anything I could do for him until the EMTs got there. They had to use the Jaws of Life to get him out. He had a massive head injury and spent weeks in the hospital in an unresponsive state."

"You know that wasn't your fault." Langston stopped the golf cart and looked at her.

"That's easy for you to say. You didn't face his parents every day. See the blame in their eyes even when they didn't say it." Her eyes remained on her clasped hands in her lap. "Or worse, be there when they turned off the machine and he was gone. I should have been able to do more. If I had known more human medicine, then I could have done something more. Maybe saved him."

Langston said the words softly as if recognizing their truth. "So you changed to human medicine, thinking you could save others like him."

Callee said nothing. Finally, Langston started

driving again. She was grateful when they arrived at the clinic. She needed some time alone. Grabbing her bag, she got off the cart. "Thanks for your help. It was nice to have it."

"Glad I could."

She started for the track.

"Not coming in?" Concern laced his words.

"I will in a few minutes." Callee kept walking. She felt Langston's gaze on her for a long time.

CHAPTER THREE

BY THE SECOND week Langston had been at the clinic, he knew he could find Callee at the track every morning. This one was no different. She stood in her usual position with her foot propped on the bottom rail. Her jeans stretched tight across her bottom. She might be petit, but she sure had curves in all the right places.

Langston couldn't help but smile. Callee had more spunk than he'd given her credit for. As small as she was, she carried a powerful personality. He'd spent most of the last few days in her office on the computer, yet he'd heard her with patients. More than once he had offered to help. She had insisted she didn't need him.

He had quickly learned Callee was a self-sufficient person. It was as if she held herself at a distance, not wanting anybody to really get to know her. He suspected what she'd told him about her past had much to do with it.

He'd looked forward to this assignment, but he'd had no idea how interesting he would find it. Working at the clinic was nothing like what he expected. When this idea had been suggested, he thought it would be rather dull. He'd had no idea when he pulled into the parking spot that first morning and noticed people lined up along the railing, that he'd find himself drawn to it each morning as well. Slowly and unexpectedly he had become one of them.

He'd never guessed there were as many head concussions in horse racing as he was finding. The number was approaching that of football. Every sport would benefit from the information he would gain here. He liked being a doctor, but he wanted to do something bigger and more significant. He would never be satisfied doing what Callee did. Having the same routine day after day in the same place. Like living in Prairie where nothing changed.

Yet when was the last time he had someone he could call a best friend? Or live in a community where his neighbors waved, or he could call them by name? So much of his adult life had been caught up in constant change. But hadn't that been what he'd wanted? To get away from the small-town-going-nowhere life? To see the world. And he had. A couple of times.

Oddly he had found the repetitive mode he'd been in for the past few days settling, reassuring. Almost pleasant. He just might miss the clinic when he left. Or was it Callee who was getting under his skin? He'd never let a woman affect his decisions one way or another again. The one time he had it had been heartbreaking.

The last of the horses ran by. Callee strolled toward the clinic. He fell in beside her. As they approached the building, he saw a group milling around the entrance. "What's going on?"

"It's Wednesday. This weekend they race. They're here for their drug test."

"You didn't say they were going to be doing those here today." If he'd known, he could have been more prepared. To have this many jockeys in one place at the same time was a gold mine of information.

"I didn't know until last night. They don't always give me much notice. The stewards send a crew here to administer the test. Oh, man, I'm sorry." She grabbed his arm. "I should have said something. This is a perfect time for you to talk to most of the jockeys. You don't have to go out and hunt them down for interviews. They have all come to you."

"Yep. My thoughts exactly. I need to get busy. I'll get my notebook. At least I can weed out the ones I don't need to talk to in-depth. Then go find those I do for more of an interview."

She shook her head. "I should have thought."

Callee acted as if she were beating herself up over a simple mistake. "It's good. No worries."

"Sometimes I just don't think." She hung her head.

His brows drew together. Was she thinking about what happened to her boyfriend? That she hadn't stopped him? Couldn't have helped him more? That she'd done something wrong?

One of the jockeys spoke to Callee, and she stepped over to him.

Langston continued inside. The real work was about to begin. A shudder of excitement went through him. He liked the detective work that went into finding the element that made the difference in changing someone's life.

He returned to the front with his notebook and pen in hand. Callee stood at the desk talking to Carl.

"I told them that I'd appreciate it if they'd talk to you," Callee offered. "I'll be out to help after I sign off on the stewards being here and make sure they have everything thing they need. But I wouldn't wait on me. The jockeys won't hang around to answer questions."

He had this. "I think I can handle it."

She smiled. "If you say so."

A man and woman entered. One carried a case. "Mornin', Callee. Sorry we're late."

Callee greeted them by name. "No problem. They're lined up for you out there."

One of the stewards said, "Yep. We'll be ready in a minute, do this thing and be out of your way."

Langston went outside. Intimated for a moment by all the eyes directed toward him. He spoke in Spanish. "Is there anyone here who has hit his head?"

Broad smiles slowly appeared on everyone's faces.

He smiled as well. "Okay, of course you have. Let's go with have you ever been knocked out."

No one moved. Finally, a man looked Langston in the eye and nodded. Then another. He looked beyond Langston.

He turned to see Callee standing nearby. A slight grin on her lips.

To the first jockey he said, "I'd like to ask you some questions about your fall."

Callee came to stand beside him. Langston had to pull the information out of the jockey, starting with his name. He told Langston about the horse throwing him three years earlier.

"Did you have trouble standing, walking, or seeing? Did you see a doctor?" The list of questions went on. Langston continued to quickly ask them until it was that jockey's turn to get his test.

During a pause in the line, Langston turned to see Callee talking to a group of men. He moved on to the next jockey who indicated he'd had a fall. An hour passed quickly. Langston managed to interview five people. Far fewer than the number of jockeys who had shown up for their tests.

"Here you go." Callee handed him a paper. "I found some you can interview."

He looked at the list. There had to be ten names and phone numbers listed. All that time he'd thought she was just socializing. "Uh...thanks. I appreciate it."

"They will have to be tested again before you leave so you can catch those you missed or who have just arrived then."

Langston dipped his chin. "This gives me a good start. I appreciate your support. I realize now I would've had a much harder time getting them to talk if it hadn't been for you."

"Sometimes arrogance doesn't work." She gave him a thin smile.

"I've been accused of that. Something about just because I'm the smartest man in the room I shouldn't tell everyone that."

She started toward the clinic door. "I can see why that would get you in trouble."

"I have a feeling you know just how to keep me in check." Callee cut to the heart of matters. He didn't have to question where he stood.

"I'll take that as a compliment."

"I'm not sure it was meant that way." Langston wasn't sure he liked Callee understanding as well as she did. "How about joining me for dinner this evening."

She cut her eyes at him. "Uh, thanks, but I can't. Tonight's my poker game. I'm a designated dessert bringer. I thought you were coming along."

She wasn't sure if she could handle having him around after-hours, but she'd issued the invitation last week and she'd stand by it. There would be others there, which was much safer than being alone at dinner."

"Who's in on this game anyway?"

"Most of them you've already met." It wasn't like him to act unsure.

"What kind of stakes are we talking about?" He flipped through his notes.

She studied him a moment. Was he looking for a way out of the game. "Mostly penny ante and bragging rights."

"I believe I can handle that. Do I need to bring anything but my wallet?" His face brightened.

"Nope. You're a guest tonight. We start at seven, next door."

A few hours later Callee knew the moment Langston arrived. Despite having her back to the door, the atmosphere in the room changed. Something about Langston drew her to him. That had to stop. It was unhealthy. Langston moved from place to place like a traveling salesman, but for the first time in a long time a man fascinated her.

She stopped her conversation with Gina to go meet him. As always, he exuded self-assurance. "Hey there. Are you ready for this?"

"I know you said not to bring anything, but I brought some chips and dip anyway."

"Thanks. You can never go wrong with those. Give them here and I'll take care of them." She placed them on the table holding the pizza and drinks.

Gina sashayed up to them. "Hi, there, Langston. I'm so glad you joined us tonight."

"Hi, Gina. How's it going with the horses these days?"

"Great."

"Let's play cards," Rick bellowed. "I have an early morning tomorrow and need to beat you all so I can go to bed."

There was a lot of scoffing and good-natured ribbing in the room while chairs were being pulled to the table.

"Should I sit anywhere special?" Langston asked Callee.

"Everyone has their usual place, but the chair across from me is empty." She would at least enjoy the view tonight.

The group settled into their seats. She quickly introduced Langston. Rick picked up an unopened card deck and broke the seal. "Five card stud is the game tonight, ladies and gents."

She hissed along with a couple of the others. "Rick, you know I prefer Texas Hold 'em."

"When it's your week to call the game, we can play that. Tonight, we're playing straight up poker." Rick shuffled the cards.

Callee looked at Langston to find him watching her. He smiled.

Rick passed out the cards. When everyone had

five apiece, he turned the deck upside down on the table.

Calle picked her cards up off the table. Fanning them out, she glanced over at Langston who did the same. Glad she hadn't sat next to him because this way she could see him. She watched his long fingers move the cards around.

Everyone anted up in the center of the table.

Since she sat to the side of Rick, she drew a card and discarded another.

The game came down to two of the eight players. One called the other, and the pot was taken.

When Langston's turn came to deal, he shuffled the cards like an expert and passed them out. His look met hers when he finished. She returned it, her skin heated.

With the first round of play over, Callee pushed back her chair. "I'm hungry. I'm going to sit this next round out."

Langston said, "I'll join you."

Rick murmured, "I'm not surprised."

Gina giggled.

She and Langston picked up a slice of pizza.

"You want a beer with that?" Langston asked, going to the cooler.

"No, thanks. I'll stick with a soft drink." She couldn't trust herself to drink after what happen to Joe.

He nodded and pulled out a can. "I thought after

working here all day you'd want to stay away in the evenings."

Callee looked at the table of people laughing and joking with each other. "These are my people."

"Do you do anything else with your time off?"

He made it sound like he thought she might be dull. "I visit my family. I also have a horse I spend time with on the weekends."

"Do you ever travel?"

"Not really. I'm mostly a homebody. I must be rather uninteresting to you since you've been all over the world." It sort of angered her she'd let him make her feel unsophisticated. Even if she might be.

"The last thing you are is uninteresting. Is there nowhere you would like to visit?" His disbelief rang in every word.

"Sure. A few." She thought of traveling but hadn't had the chance. Still, she didn't deserve that kind of fun either. She and Joe had made plans for vacations. Ones that he never had a chance to experience.

"Like where?"

Why was this so important to Langston?

"Hey, y'all gonna play or not?" Rick called.

"I'm playing." Callee threw the last of her pizza in the trash.

"I want to hear your answer later." Langston brought his beer with him.

"Okay." Her eyes narrowed on the can. She

wouldn't let herself spend her poker evening counting others' drinks. Judging others' habits wasn't what she wanted to do.

An hour went by with her watching Langston and him watching her. He had the most amazing eyes. Such a beautiful blue.

"Hey, Callee, when can we have some of those brownies?" Gina asked from where she sat next to Langston.

"Help yourself." Callee tried to concentrate on her cards.

Gina looked at Langston and smiled. "Can't I get you one?"

"Sure."

Gina put her hand on Langston's shoulder and pushed herself to standing. "This is a tight table." She grinned at Callee.

Trying not to react, Callee watched Gina walk away. Her friend was working to get a response out of her. She had no plans to give one.

Gina returned with a plate filled with brownies. She smiled sweetly at Langston. "I thought we could share."

Rick huffed.

Langston took one of the dark chocolate squares and bit into it. "Mmm. This is really good."

Callee smirked at him. "Don't act so surprised."

"Callee calls it her secret recipe," Gina said, giving her friend a wink.

Langston raised his hand with the brownie in it. "My compliments to the chef."

Heat washed through her.

"Are you two going to make moony eyes at each other or play cards?" Rick sounded disgusted.

Callee pretended to focus on her cards.

"Why wouldn't I want to look at a pretty woman?" Langston quipped.

A rumble of laughs circled the table.

She glanced at Langston. His grin reached his eyes.

"Just play cards," Rick grumbled.

They played another couple of hours before two people at the table pushed back their chairs. "Race day tomorrow. Time to go. The morning will come quick."

"Yeah, it's time I call it a day too." Callee stood and stretched. She started cleaning up; Gina joined her.

"You like him, don't you?" Gina said.

"Who?" Callee tried to sound as if she didn't know what her friend meant.

Gina bumped her shoulder against Callee's. "Come on. It's me you're talking to. Rick isn't the only one who saw all that eye contact."

"There was no eye contact. We're just friends." Callee couldn't start thinking like that.

"I know how friends look at each other. Langston didn't taken his eyes off you all evening. And they weren't 'just friends' looks." Gina threw an empty pizza box away.

Langston had been watching her, but she wasn't going to admit it. "You're nuts."

"I think you need to open your eyes, so to speak. Have a little fun, Callee, you deserve it. You shouldn't punish yourself all your life. Think about it. You never know what you might miss out on." Gina picked up her purse.

Rick called, "Night, Callee."

"Bye, Rick. Better luck next week."

Langston stepped up beside her. "What's the deal with that guy?"

"He's jealous," Gina offered.

Callee gasped. "He is not."

Gina shot back, "He's sweet on you and you know it." She grinned and headed toward the door. "I'd better catch my ride back with the boys."

"If you're ready, Callee, I'll walk you to your car," Langston said. "So you and Rick?"

"That's just Gina talking. You do know I can get to my car on my own without any trouble."

"I'm sure you can, but I want to finish our conversation." He dumped the empty chip bag and leftover dip in the garbage.

"Why does it matter whether I'd like to travel?"

He shrugged. "I don't know. I guess because I don't understand you not being more interested in seeing the world. My father and mother are like that. I never understood it. They're happy in the same old house, in the same old town, with the same old people."

"Is that a bad thing?"

He thought for a moment. "Not bad. More like a sad one."

"Are they unhappy people?" She headed for the door with the glass brownie dish in her hand.

"Well, no." He followed her.

"Everyone has a way they want to live. Apparently, that isn't yours." She pushed the door open.

"Never thought about it like that. I've always seen it as scared to do something different."

What must he think of her lifestyle? "Is that why you stay on the go so much? Because you don't want to be like your parents?"

"I love my parents. They were good ones, but yes, I guess that's it. I just wanted more." He took the dish then waited while she locked up.

A darkness entered his eyes before he answered. Was there more to his running than his parents' lifestyle example? Her words where sharper than she intended. "Or what you believe is more. How many close friends do you have? How often do you see your apartment? Sleep in your own bed?"

Langston raised a hand. "Okay, okay you've made your point."

"I'm sorry. That didn't sound very nice."

He walked beside her. "You don't mind saying what you're thinking, do you?"

"Not usually. But I shouldn't be mean."

Langston walked within touching distance but didn't even brush her arm. "I want to know what you think. Too often women try to tell me what I want to hear."

"I bet they do," she murmured.

"What do you mean by that?"

"Come on. You know you're an attractive man with a good job. You're a real catch in today's dating world." Callee put a little laugh in her voice.

"Thanks. But with those accolades you still don't want me." He made it sound as if he were teasing her, but there was a ring of truth in there too.

"I didn't say that." They had reached her car.

"Because we don't agree on how to live our lives." His statement was matter-of-fact.

She placed a hand on his arm. "Maybe not, but that doesn't mean we can't be friends."

A smile came to his face. "Agreed. That was fun tonight. Thanks for inviting me. It's been a long time since I just hung out with some people."

"You should get another chance before you have to leave." She was becoming too attached to Langston. He would be gone soon. Then what would she have? She took the dish from him and placed it inside her car.

Callee remembered he'd been drinking. She couldn't let him drive home. Would never forgive herself if something happened to him. Like Joe. She wouldn't live though another experience like that. "Hey, Langston. Leave your truck here. I'll drive you home."

He chuckled. "In that clown car? I am well over six feet."

She looked at him. "I guess you would have to ride with your feet over the windshield."

"I probably could, but it doesn't sound like much fun. But I can see that it's a perfect size for you." He gave her a sweeping look she suspected had nothing to do with fitting into her car.

"Then I'll drive your truck," she announced.

He huffed. "Callee, I got this."

"I'd prefer to drive you home. I'm going to insist." She put out her hand for the keys.

"Okay. If that'll make you happy, but it isn't necessary." He handed her his keys.

"It is to me." She started toward his truck. "You coming?"

He slapped his hat against his jean-covered leg. "I'm not sure whether to be disgusted or flattered you care."

"I'm just being a responsible adult." Unlike what she had been years ago.

Understanding washed over his face. "I get it. This has to do with what happen to your boyfriend."

"No. It has to do with not letting friends drive when they've drank too much." Her defense sounded harsher than it should.

"I think you are overreacting, but I'm too tired

to argue with you. Can you handle a real vehicle after driving that toy car?"

She grinned. "You just buckle up and watch."

Langston did. And enjoyed the show. Callee had to work to get up into the driver's seat of the high truck. He didn't miss a movement of her twist and turns. This ride home might not be a bad idea after all.

He hurried around the truck and got in on the passenger side. The truck rumbled to life. When Callee grinned at him, he returned it.

The entire evening he had watched her. Rick had been right. Langston had been fixated on her mouth. One minute she was biting her bottom lip, then the next she was sucking on it. All he could think about was how much he wanted to kiss that tender sweet flesh Callee kept worrying.

She backed up, and headed out to the main road. "Which way?"

"I'm over in the Newport area," he said, watching her profile as they went down the road.

She glanced at him. "Wow, high cotton."

"I'm in a corporate apartment." One that looked just like the one before it, and the one before that.

"That sounds better than a hotel."

He nodded. "It is. I've done one of those too often."

"You don't ever get tired of not sleeping in your own bed?" She merged on to the freeway.

"Not so far." How much longer would it be before he did?

"I wouldn't like that. I like my bed."

He imagined her waiting on him in that bed. "Make a right here."

Callee took it a little fast and the tires squealed. She grinned at him. "I need to have some fun."

He leaned back toward the window so he could see her more clearly and draped an arm across the back of the seat. "Go for it."

She grinned. "It's been a long time since I've driven a truck. I forgot how superior it makes you feel."

His brows came together. "Was there a slam on me in there?"

"Depends." Her focus didn't leave the road.

"On what?"

"On your driving. I accuse men in big trucks who drive too fast and tailgate of using their trucks to compensate for their lack of size elsewhere."

"Ouch, that hurts." He dropped his voice into a low stern tone. "I can assure you I don't drive fast or tailgate, and as for the size of my truck…that isn't the case for me."

"I bet that's what they all say," she teased.

He just gave a wry smile, wanting more than anything the opportunity to prove her theory wrong to her.

"The gated community ahead is it. I'm in H building." He pointed toward his building. She drove to where he had instructed her. "Pull into parking spot twenty-three. That's mine."

Callee parked and turned off the engine. She shifted to look at him. Behind the wheel of the large truck, she seemed almost like a child.

"Do you mind if I drive your truck home and pick you up in the morning?"

He unbuckled. "I was wondering if you had thought through how you were going to get home."

"I hadn't but I have a plan now." She looked at his building.

"How about coming in for a cup of coffee? I think I can get one of those together."

Her lips formed a thin line. "Don't tell me you're one of those people who has an empty refrigerator."

"Tread carefully, Callee. You've already insulted my manhood. You don't want to do it twice."

She smiled slightly. "Okay. I'll behave."

"What time should I expect you in the morning?"

"Five."

"Okay. I'll be ready." He climbed out of the truck. Before she could leave the parking space, he walked to her door.

She lowered the window and leaned out. "You forget something?"

"I did. A thank you for caring enough to bring me home."

His mouth brushed hers, oh so softly. Callee's

lips were as plush and warm as he had imagined. Could a kiss be any sweeter?

She leaned out the window, returning the touch. "You're welcome. Anytime."

He grinned. "See you in the morning, sweet Callee."

CHAPTER FOUR

CALLEE WAITED NERVOUSLY the next morning in Langston's truck while he strolled down the sidewalk from his apartment. Unfortunately, she had to pick him up and was forced to sit in a confined space with him so soon after their kiss. Her lips were still tingling and her heart beat faster with just the thought of it.

She'd been kissed before but none had left her reeling at the memory. And it had been only a tiny touch of the lips, but she'd relived that moment all night long. With a mixture of eagerness and reluctance, she looked forward to seeing Langston. To being kissed again.

Callee shouldn't allow another kiss or herself to think like that. She didn't deserve that exhilaration. She hadn't earned that type of happiness.

"Good mornin'," Langston cheerfully said as she scooted over and he climbed behind the wheel of the truck.

"Hi."

He acted so unaffected by their kiss she thought about insulting his manhood to get a reaction. She resisted the urge.

They had a quiet drive to the track. She felt him

watching her, but he'd always looked away by the time she could look at him. Langston pulled into his usual parking spot, and they climbed out.

"What's going on today? Something I need to know about?" Langston looked around. "I can't get over all this activity."

Callee stared at him. He was clueless. "It's a race day. We usually race Thursday through Sunday here.

"I assumed they only ran here on Derby Weekend."

"A lot of people think that. Churchill Downs hosts the Kentucky Derby on the first Saturday in May but there are races here almost year-round. The horses have to qualify, so there's races all over the country. Regular race days here are exciting, but they're nothing compared to Derby Weekend."

"I didn't know any of that. I should've done my homework." His tone implied he truly wished he had.

"I suspect the reason why has to do with your work. You don't take notice." She walked toward the track.

"Do you really think I'm that narrow-minded? That I don't appreciate anything but my work?" His voice held a note of disappointment.

She pursed her lips. "It's more like focused."

"You have to work hard to get ahead." He sounded determined.

"That's what's most important to you?" She watched him.

"I would like to make a difference in the world, yes."

Callee stuffed her hands in the front pockets of her jeans. "That's commendable. But the small things add up too."

He appeared to give that some thought.

Callee took her usual place beside the fence. She glanced back at Langston. He stepped up beside her but not too close. She stilled, too aware of his long body. Her look dropped to his lips. Did he remember their kiss like she did? If he kissed her again, what would she do?

She wouldn't let that happen. That needed to remain fixed in her mind.

The horses had just run by when she glanced over her shoulder at the clinic. "Rick!"

She hurried to the clinic where her friend waited in front of the door, his shoulder covered in blood. Inside she led him down the hall toward an exam room. "Come this way, Rick."

Langston had entered the clinic right behind her. He waited in the hallway.

Somehow, she had to get beyond the jitters she had at just the thought of Langston.

"What's going on with Rick?" Langston demanded when she came out into the hall.

"He has a nasty bite on his shoulder." She hurried to the supply closet.

Langston brows rose. "Bite?"

"Horse bite." She placed supplies in his hands when he offered.

"Really?"

"Yeah, it happens more often than you would think." She handed him another box.

"Gold Star is notorious for it." Rick stood in the doorway.

Langston studied the man a moment. "That looks painful."

Rick said, "It is."

"Then I think you should sit down." Langston urged Rick back into the examination room by walking toward him.

Callee came in behind them. "Rick, when was the last time you had a tetanus shot?"

The man groaned. "I don't know but I hate needles."

"I'll have Carl check your file. If you need the shot, you'll have to have one ASAP." Callee put the supplies down and faced her patient. "Come on, tough guy. I need to get that shirt off you. Someone who works with animals as large as a horse all day shouldn't be afraid of a little old needle."

"What happened to a woman showing tender loving care, instead of making fun of a man? If you'd go out with me, you'd find I'm nothing more than a marshmallow."

"Do you mind helping me with this?" She

looked at Langston. He wore a frown and glared at Rick.

"Not at all." Langston stepped closer to examine the wound, going into doctor mode.

Callee spoke to Rick. "The skin has been broken so we'll clean it good and see if it needs any stitches. It's pretty mangled."

"This isn't the first time Gold Star has gotten me, but it's the worst." Rick winced as she worked his shirt off.

"I hate to say it, but we're going to need to cut the sleeve off. It's stuck to the wound." Langston picked up the scissors. "We should also do an X-ray of the shoulder socket. There may be damaged to it." Langston lifted Rick's arm, rotating it.

Callee watched Rick's face. He grimaced. She said to Rick, "Come on, big guy." She took his arm. "Let's take a walk down the hall."

Langston didn't follow. "I'll finish getting supplies together."

By the time they had returned, Langston had assembled the saline, suture kit and bandages.

"If you'll pour the saline, I'll hold the pan," Callee said to Langston.

Minutes later they had the site clean.

"Rick, we're going to do some picking around here. We need to make sure the site is absolutely clean. If not, we could just bandage up germs to fester."

Rick released a heavy sigh. "Okay."

Using tweezers, she moved the damaged skin to see beneath it.

Langston stepped closer using his penlight. "Look right there. Isn't that something?"

"Good catch." She smiled at Langston. He returned one that reached his eyes. "It looks like a piece of oat. Rick, we're going to need to do some more washing so don't move."

Langston opened another bottle of saline. She held the pan as he poured. Finished, she studied the site once more. Callee bumped her head against Langston's as she stood. She looked up to find a silly grin on his face. Her heart did a little flip-flop. She liked that one far more than the expression earlier.

"Rick, it looks clean this time. No stitches, but you'll have a nasty scar." She took a tube of ointment and applied it to each mark on Rick's arm.

Langston then applied the gauze bandage, moving around the arm and over the shoulder and back until it was secure.

"All right, you're all done, Rick." Callee stepped back and looked at him. "I'd like to see you back on Monday for a bandage change. No getting in the stall with Gold Star. This must stay clean."

Rick stood. "You know you could keep a closer check on me if you went out with me."

Callee gave him a nudge on his good arm. "Enough of that."

Langston stayed behind to clean up while Callee walked Rick out.

When she returned Langston said, "That guy was hitting on you."

A little thrill went through her. Langston had noticed. "Rick always talks like that. He doesn't mean anything by it."

"You might be surprised. You're an attractive, single woman. What makes you think he's not interested?"

Langston thought she was pretty. She savored that knowledge. "Maybe the fact he hasn't seriously asked me out."

"Would you go?" Langston watched her too closely for her comfort.

"Probably not."

Langston stepped out of the room with a hand full of unused supplies then returned. "Why isn't someone as amazing as you married, or at least have a boyfriend?"

"I could ask you the same thing. Why isn't there a Mrs. Watts or at least a girlfriend?"

"There was to be one. But she decided on another guy. My best friend, Mark."

Callee's eyes widened. She sucked in a breath.

What made him say that? He didn't talk about what happened between him and Emily. And Mark. "Also, because I'm never in one place long enough to have a relationship anymore. That's certainly not your problem. As far as I can tell, your entire world is this place."

What point was he trying to make? "Are you encouraging me to go out with Rick?"

His mouth formed a hard line. "I am not. If anything, I'd like you to go out with me."

Callee hadn't expected that declaration. She looked at him for a moment. "Okay, Wandering Man, I'll call your bluff. I have to attend the Derby Ball week after next."

He grinned. "Then it's a date, Stay Put Woman."

With only two weeks until the Derby, the backside was already busier than it had been when Langston arrived. Trucks pulling trailers filled with horses were arriving daily. The barns were occupied almost to capacity with horses. Trainers were working the horses on the track all day. Exercise boys were busy walking and bathing the horses while grooms and stable hands cleaned the stalls and equipment. All this leading up to Derby Week.

He stepped beside Callee at the track railing early that morning. Speaking in a quiet voice he said, "What's going on? You look nervous."

"Gina is riding this morning. She's super excited."

Langston had started to recognize Callee's moods. He'd never really bothered to do so with anyone else. She was becoming too familiar. He had no idea what he was doing, but just couldn't help himself. He found Callee irresistible. He'd like to call it an impulse to kiss her the other day, but that would be a lie. He'd been thinking about repeating it almost constantly.

He would be leaving in a few weeks, which meant he'd probably never see her again. That idea made him pause. Why did that bother him? He'd dated plenty of women short term and never had a problem. Why couldn't Callee fall into that same category?

In the past he had always been ready to leave when the time came, but the idea bothered him this time for some reason. He had become too attached to the place. Attached to Callee.

Langston grinned. He would have her all to himself at the Derby Ball in another week. It would be nice to get her away from the clinic. That was all she seemed to focus on. Who was he to talk? His work was his life.

Callee's phone rang. Her face blanched. "Don't move her. Call 911. I'm on the way." She looked at him in wide-eyed panic.

"What's wrong?"

"Gina's been thrown while still in the starting gate. She's unconscious." Callee looked as if she didn't know what to do first.

"My bag's in my truck. Let's go." He took her hand, directing her toward his truck.

They ran the short distance and climbed in. As

soon as she had closed the door, he started the engine and backed up.

"Take the tunnel under the track. It'll bring us up close to the gates." Callee sat with her hands clutched in her lap.

Langston took a second to place his hand over hers. "She's going to be fine."

Callee stared straight ahead.

His chest tightened. He hoped he had told the truth.

"Turn into the tunnel here." Callee directed him to the left. "Make a right when you come out. Drive along the rail."

"Gotcha."

"Gina was the first person to accept me when I moved here. I needed her to do that. It hadn't been long after Joe's death." She talked more to herself than to him. "She got me to talk about what happened. Just listened and didn't judge. She helped me believe in myself again. She took time to introduce me around. Make me feel a part of this place. Became the friend that I needed. I can't lose her too." The last few words were close to being sobs.

Langston hated he couldn't put an arm around Callee and comfort her. Clearly any head injury she came across immediately conjured in her mind an outcome just like Joe's. Despite Gina's help, Callee had a way to go before completely accepting what happen to her boyfriend.

He drove into the daylight and turned.

She pushed to the edge of the seat, pointed out the window. "Right down there. On the track. Hurry."

Langston drove as fast as he dared. Moments later he pulled to a stop across from the rail where the large metal starting gate sat on the track. Behind it a group of people encircled Gina, who lay on the ground.

Callee was out of the truck before he pulled to a full stop. By the time he reached the rail, she was on the other side and running toward the group. Langston followed with his medical bag in hand.

"What happened?" Callee demanded as she went down on a knee to examine Gina.

"Gold Star was being temperamental this morning. We were having difficulty getting him into the gate. Gina said she could handle him, but the moment the gate opened he reared. Gina was wearing a helmet, but she hit her head so hard on the back gate the helmet split."

That horse again. First Rick and now Gina. When did a trainer say the horse was too dangerous?

Langston asked, "Has 911 been called?"

Someone in the crowd yelled, "Yes. An ambulance is on the way."

Langston dropped to his knees across from Callee. He made a mental note that one of the policies for all track personal should be training on emergency care of head injuries. "We need a blanket here."

He glanced at Callee. Her eyes swam with tears. As the most experienced with this type of injury and the expert here, he should take the lead. In a stern voice he said, "Callee, I have this. This is my area of expertise. Go hold Gina's feet up to prevent shock while someone gets something for them to rest on." He barked out an order to a nearby man.

She looked at him a second. Finally, her eyes focused. She then stood and did as he had told her.

Pulling the penlight out of his pocket, he lifted Gina's eyelids. They were fixed and dilated. He set the helmet to the side, and said to no one in particular, "This needs to go to the hospital with her."

Then Langston pulled a neck brace out of his go-bag. Gently he worked it around Gina's neck. Someone put a blanket within his eyesight, and he placed it over Gina's chest. With his fingertips he carefully examined the back of her head, looking for bumps or indentions.

A man hurried forward with a low step and handed it to Callee. She slipped it under Gina's feet, then returned to Langston's side. She said in a controlled voice, "I'll do vitals."

"I can use your help." Langston was proud of her strength. He moved his hands along Gina's shoulders and arms, looking for any breaks.

Callee checked her heart, blood pressure and other vitals.

"Don't move her legs," Langston snapped to a man near Gina. "She might have a spinal injury."

The sound of an ambulance pierced the air. Moments later it quietly entered the space between the stands and the track fence, then stopped at the open gate. The EMTs rolled a stretcher over the red clay surface.

"Callee, give the report." That would give her something to focus on instead of worrying about Gina. "I'll be going with Gina."

"Okay." Her eyes still looked watery.

He wanted to take her into his arms, but his focus needed to stay on Gina.

With a straight back, Callee went to meet the EMTs.

Quickly they had Gina on the stretcher and headed to the ambulance. Langston gathered his bag and hurried toward his truck. Callee was right beside him.

He climbed in. She stopped him from closing the door with a hand on his arm. "You'll keep me posted on what's going on. How she is."

He took her hand and squeezed it. "Of course, I will."

"I can't leave the clinic." Agony filled her eyes.

He nodded. "I'll let you know everything I know. You can get a ride back?"

"Don't worry about that. I'll get one of those guys to take me. Go take care of Gina."

"Consider it done." Langston gave her a reassuring smile. He intended to keep his promise.

Callee arrived at the hospital as soon after the clinic closed as she could. Langston had kept her posted on how Gina was progressing. He had been as good as his word. He'd texted almost hourly. By the time Langston had arrived at the hospital, Gina had regained consciousness.

He instructed Callee to text him when she got to the hospital, and he would meet her. She had never been so glad to see someone as she had when Langston stalked toward her in the hospital lobby. He opened his arms and she walked into them. Those strong arms pulled her close. She wrapped hers around his waist. She pressed her ear against his chest and listened to the steady reassuring beat of his heart.

Langston kissed the top of her head. "She should be fine. They're going to keep her in ICU for observation for tonight."

"I was so scared."

"I know, honey."

"I wasn't much help. What kind of medical person am I if I can't even help my best friend?"

"The best kind. You have a big heart. Now clear up that face. Gina is expecting you. Her parents should be here soon." He released her and took her hand. It felt right there. "This way."

"That was my first time handling a head injury since Joe."

"I thought it must be by your reaction. You do know that not every head injury ends in a bad result?"

"The ones I'm familiar with do. Joe was in a coma, he never regained consciousness. His parents had to make the decision to take him off life support."

"That is tough." He squeezed her shoulders.

"They blamed me. Wouldn't let me see him. Even to say goodbye."

"People don't always act nice when their emotions are involved."

"I needed training then. I need more now."

"I made a note that the track needs more training for everyone." He led her to the elevators. "Too many times people with no knowledge are the ones on the scene first. The right helmets are important too."

"Thank goodness Gina was wearing one."

The door opened and they stepped onto the elevator. "Yeah, but it wasn't one of ours and it split. That shouldn't have happened."

They arrived at ICU to learn they had taken Gina down for an MRI. Langston directed Callee to a small waiting room. The nurse had said she would come get them when Gina returned.

"I'm glad you were here when she woke. Someone she knew. Her family lives in California. She doesn't really have anybody but me around here. Thank you."

Langston took her hand again. She liked having hers in his. It felt strong and secure. As he spoke, he played with her fingers. "Hey, that wasn't a problem. Hopefully Gina will see us in a little bit."

"I'm glad they're keeping her in the hospital overnight. They need to make sure she's okay."

"I thought it was for the best."

Callee looked at him in surprise. "You're her doctor?"

He nodded. "I'm one of them."

"You have privileges here?" She continued to watch him.

"I told you I fill in some when I travel. I have temporary privileges in one hospital in every city I'm living in. It makes it easier if something like this happens. I also do research in hospitals. Or in this case have my own patient."

"That makes sense. I'm impressed."

He grinned. "I'm glad to hear it. I wasn't sure I could impress you. Just the other day you were mad at me."

"Yeah, but you shouldn't—"

Langston gave her a quick kiss. "I shouldn't have brought it up."

"Are you going to kiss me every time I mention it to shut me up?"

"I might. I'll just have to see."

She would be disappointed if he didn't.

A nurse walked toward them. "Dr. Watts, she's back. The test results you wanted are posted as well."

Langston rose and offered Callee a hand. She placed hers in his, and he helped her to her feet.

"I'm going to check those results. The nurse will show you to Gina. I'll meet you there."

Callee joined the nurse.

"Your friend has one of the best trauma doctors in the country. He's brilliant. We're honored to have him in our department even for a short time."

Callee had no idea. Langston had played down his credentials.

"Here you go. She's right here. I know she's anxious to see you." The nurse showed her to a corner room.

Callee entered the glass-enclosed room to find Gina sitting up in bed but looking pale. Callee hurried to the bed. "Hey, how are you doing? You're not looking too much worse for wear."

Gina offered a weak smile. "I don't feel too bad. Just a little unsteady when they let me walk. Which isn't often."

"Then I suggest you don't walk. Take advantage of the help around here." Callee touched Gina's hand. "You scared me."

"Sorry. I didn't intend to. I've had a lot of attention today. Especially Langston's. Did you know he was such a rock star in the medical world?"

"No, he never mentioned it." Why hadn't he?

"I'll admit he was pretty nice to wake up to. The problem is he only wants to talk about you." Gina smirked as she watched her friend closely.

Callee blushed. "I seriously doubt that."

"Is there something going on that I should know about?"

"Nothing other than we're going to the Derby Ball together." Callee looked at the floor not wanting to meet Gina's look.

She grinned. "I think there's more than that."

There were those few quick kisses. But so brief they couldn't have meant anything. "Believe what you like. Enough about me. How does your head feel?"

"Pretty good. I'm not sure why they're making me stay here overnight, but Langston insisted."

Callee wasn't surprised. "He has a habit of getting his way."

"Callee, he's a good guy."

"Yeah, he kind of proved his worth today." Callee appreciated Langston's steady hand when she'd been so shaken. She couldn't have survived the loss of another friend.

"Thanks," Langston's deep voice said from behind her. "I'm glad I came in when I did."

"Don't let your ego get carried away," Callee quipped.

He stepped up beside her. "Watch it. My feelings can be hurt."

Callee looked at him. "All you have to do is step out in the hall and the nurses are all agog."

"Excuse me, patient here." Gina pointed to herself.

"Yes, you are." Langston looked at her. "Do you still have a headache?"

"Yes." Gina touched her head.

"It should get better slowly. If it gets worse, I want you to let the nurse know immediately."

"I will." Gina looked at Callee. "Instead of hovering over me, why don't you two go out to dinner? I'll be right here when you get back."

"I think I need to stay here with you." Even injured Gina was busy matchmaking.

"My parents will be here soon. Anyway, they're going to kick you out soon. Go on. I'd like to take a nap."

Callee pointed a finger at her. "Okay, but I'm going to have the nurse call me if you don't do exactly what they say."

She and Langston walked down the hall toward the elevators. "Do you mind if we get takeout? I don't generally do that when I take a lady out, but I am hungry and not up to waiting at a restaurant."

"We don't have to go to dinner together. That's just Gina trying to matchmake."

"As far as I'm concerned, she's wasting her efforts." He pushed the button for the elevator.

A sadness washed over Callee. She'd been right. Those kisses had meant nothing.

Langston gaze met hers. "Because I'm already interested."

Callee swallowed the lump that had formed in her throat. She smiled.

"Now that's settled, how about some food." He named a local chain.

"Sure." She would agree to almost anything Langston said this evening. He'd cared for her best friend and said some sweet words to her.

"Then I'll drive. I'll take you home and pick you up in the morning. We can check on Gina before going to the clinic. Do you think you can miss a breeze?"

"I can for Gina."

He led her out of the hospital to his truck.

As he drove out of the parking lot, Callee said, "I appreciate you being there for Gina today. Staying all day. I hate that I couldn't help more."

"I'm glad I could be here." He made a lane change.

"One of the nurses said you're a big deal in the head trauma world. Why didn't you tell me?"

"How was I supposed to say that without sounding insufferable? That certainly wouldn't have been the way to get your cooperation. Or earn your respect."

"Still, you could have said something." She studied his profile.

He glanced at her. "Would it have made a difference?"

"Probably not."

"I hate that Gina got hurt, but she sure did give me a nice case study. One from start to finish. As I mentioned, she wasn't wearing one of our helmets. I'm all about making one stronger, better fitting and light. But people have to wear them."

"At least she had something on. If she hadn't, she would have been sanctioned for it. Could even have lost her job. The racetrack promotes safety in every aspect. For both people and the horses."

Langston glanced at her. "You know I'll have to report all the details of the accident."

"I understand. Gina is going to be okay?"

He reached across the seat and took her hand. "I believe so. So far there haven't been any indications that there's any brain malfunctions. Other than that knot on the back of her head and being unconscious for a while, Gina doesn't appear to have any lingering issues. All the tests have come back normal."

"That's a relief." Callee rested her head against the back of the seat and closed her eyes. She took a moment to memorize the feel of her hand in Langston's. There might not be many more of those. Somewhere during the day she had decided she would take all she could get from him as long as he was around to give it.

CHAPTER FIVE

CALLEE RELAXED AS Langston pulled into the drive-through of the agreed upon hamburger place. It made her happy being with him. He placed their order and drove around the building to pick it up. A female teen gave him a broad smile when he said thanks.

"Do all the females you meet fawn over you?"

"All of them but you." He placed their food between them on the seat. "With you I've had to work at it. But it makes it so much sweeter when you earn something you've had to worked for."

"I won't ever fawn over you." She refused to.

His gaze met hers. "That's not really what I want."

"What do you want?" He had her attention now.

He didn't immediately answer. "I want you to want me as much as I do you."

"Oh."

"Does that shock you?" He stopped for a red light and looked at her. "You should know as well as I do that there's been something between us since day one."

"I don't know about that." Liar.

"Then you're fooling yourself," he said. "Gina sees it. Rick too."

She sat straighter. "Rick?"

"Yeah, he did all that talking about going out with him because he could see the electricity between us." The light changed and Langston drove on.

"I don't believe you." But she was afraid he told the truth.

"About the electricity or Rick?"

This conversation had turned uncomfortable. "Both."

"Closing your mind to it doesn't mean it isn't so. I know you're scared. That your last real relationship ended sadly, but that doesn't mean you shouldn't be happy ever again."

Thank goodness they were almost to her house. This frank discussion made her nervous. "You need to turn left at the next light. Then take the next right. I'm the third house on the right. There's a horse on the mailbox."

"Why am I not surprised."

"Don't you like horses?" She couldn't imagine life without her horse PG.

"It's not that I don't like them, it's that I don't have any experience with them." Langston pulled into her driveway.

"You don't ride?"

He turned off the truck. "No. Never had a reason to learn."

"Then you need to learn. It's like swimming, everyone needs to know how."

His chin lowered and his face turned unsure. "I don't know."

"Now who's scared?" Callee gathered the food and climbed out of the truck.

Langston met her with the drinks in hand. "It's not being scared. It's more about not having the opportunity."

"Maybe I can take you out to the farm and teach you. Between now and the Derby, I have to be at the clinic. But when things settle down we'll try." She unlocked the front door and entered.

Langston followed. "Maybe."

Callee turned on a lamp then walked into the kitchen. "Come on back here to the kitchen table. I hate eating in my lap."

He had lagged behind her. Stepping into the kitchen, he stopped. "Wow, this isn't what I expected."

Callee looked at him from where she pulled food out of the bag at the table.

"It's so, uh…feminine." Disbelief hung in the air.

She grinned. "I am a girl."

"Yeah, I've noticed. But I've never seen you in anything but practical shirts, jeans and boots to walk in on floral pillows, cushy furniture and pastel colors. I'm just a little surprised. And this kitchen looks like a chef lives here."

She laughed. "I'm not sure if I should be hurt or pleased. And I like to cook."

Langston placed the drinks beside the food and took her hand, looking into her eyes. "I'd never hurt you intentionally. A man likes a woman to surprise him every once in a while."

A shot of warmth went thought her. Langston was charming her, and she liked it too much. She pulled her hand back. "I thought you were hungry. Let's eat."

He ran a finger over the tablecloth with such care she wished he'd been touching her. "On this pretty cloth?"

Callee mentally shook herself. "I'll get us some plates and something to drink." She hurried to the cabinet and returned, setting a plate in front of him and one at her usual spot. She returned to the table. "Have a seat."

Langston took the chair to the right of her. His knees hit hers as he pushed under the table. She moved her feet so that there was room for his long legs. They passed out the food and started eating.

Callee sat back. "Where are you going after you leave here?"

Langston finished his bite. "I'm head back to Houston to compile my notes from the places I've been studying. I also have a head trauma conference to attend."

"Will you be presenting at the conference?"

"I will." He continued eating.

"Do you like to do that sort of thing?" She fingered the napkin in her lap.

He shrugged. "I like knowing that what I've learned and shared can save someone's life."

She caught his gaze. "You're a good guy, Langston Watts."

His smile reached his eyes. "Thank you. That's nice to hear."

They continued to eat. The silence wasn't uncomfortable, instead a companionable one. When they'd finished, they cleaned the table.

He looked toward the kitchen area. "You wouldn't happen to have some of those brownies around like the ones you made the other night?"

"No, but I have some chocolate chip cookies. Would you like some?"

He grinned, looking like an eager kid. "I sure would."

She went to the cookie jar. Would he make a comment about it looking like a bouquet? She opened the top and offered the cookies. He peered inside, smiled and looked at her. "May I have more than one?"

"Sure you can."

He grabbed a handful.

Callee put the container on the counter. "Let's go sit in the cushy chairs."

"You're not going to let me forget that are you?"

She grinned, shaking her head. "Probably not."

Langston took a bite of a cookie. "Mmm. These might be the best thing I've ever eaten."

She laughed. "Now you are exaggerating."

Langston eased into the love seat. "I am not. I could fall in love with you over these."

Callee knew he was kidding, but just the thought of enjoying time with a man who appreciated her and said so would be nice. She moved to sit in one of the chairs.

He patted the cushion. "Come sit beside me and I'll share my cookies with you."

She moved to the corner putting as much distance between them as possible. Not because she didn't trust him, but herself. "I only want one."

"Good. Because I didn't really want to share." He grinned as he protected the cookies against his chest.

"There are plenty."

He gave her a serious look. "Who taught you to cook?"

She gave him a direct look. "I bake."

"Bake then."

She took a bite of the cookie he offered her. "Mostly myself by trial and error."

"Not your mother?"

She shook her head. "She tried to keep me in the kitchen, but I liked the animals too much. I was always off with my father. There was no time or energy for anything more."

"You enjoyed that time."

"I loved it. I like what I do, but I also loved working with the animals." Even she heard the wistfulness in her voice.

"Or maybe it was more about the time you were spending with your father."

She never thought about it like that. "Maybe it was."

"Is there anything you don't do well? You're great with patients, horses and cooking."

"A lot. I don't speak Spanish like I wish I could."

He devoured another cookie. "I could teach you."

"What? A crash course before you go?"

He shrugged. "That and maybe some over the phone lessons. We'll start now." He picked up her hand and placed it on his head. "*El cabeza.* Say it after me."

"*El cabeza.* Head."

"*Pierna.*" He took her hand and lay it on his thigh.

Her fingers itched to massage the hard muscles beneath the jean material. "Leg."

The air around her thickened. She forced out the word. "*Pierna.*"

"Good. Now, *el corazón.*" He placed her hand beneath his over his heart. "Heart."

She repeated the word while feeling the heavy beats of his heart.

"You just have to practice them now." He abruptly let go of her hand. "Tomorrow, I'll give you a few more to work on. By the time I leave you should have a nice vocabulary."

He watched her for a long moment before he stood. "I better go."

"Uh, okay." Why the sudden change in him? She walked him to the door. "Thanks for going above the call of duty for Gina today. It means a lot to me. It was really nice to know you were there for her when I couldn't be." On an impulse gave him a kiss on the cheek.

"No problem. But I think you can do better than that little peck on the cheek." He took a step closer. "Will you please kiss me, Callee? Like you mean it."

She met his deep look, one of hope and desire. She took a step forward, reached around his neck and went up on her toes. Her lips met his. The sugar and chocolate from the cookies mingled with the taste of Langston, which made the experience heady.

Seconds later Langston's arms wrapped her waist and pulled her against his hard body.

Callee eased the kiss. Langston made a grumble of complaint before she nipped at his bottom lip then caressed it with the tip of her tongue. She asked and gained entrance to his mouth. He was eagerly waiting. His arms tightened, taking over the kisses.

Callee was immediately transported to a sphere of sensation she'd never experienced. One she didn't just want to visit but bask in. Langston's desire was a hard bulge pressed against her.

He released her mouth and put the smallest amount of space between them. "As much as I'd enjoy taking this further, it has been a long emotional day for both of us. I think I better go before I can't. Walk me to the truck."

Callee's knees were weak, but she made it to the truck. There she stopped and looked at him. She had become far too attached to a man who would be gone in a few weeks. She poked the fire of heartache. Langston was a wandering soul. He wouldn't be happy in the same place. She'd never live like a vagabond. How could they ever have more than what they had right now? Still, the man made her feel sweet things she wanted for as long as she could have them.

"Until next time." He gave her a quick kiss on the lips.

"You're mighty sure of yourself."

He grinned. "I am."

The next morning, they stopped by the hospital early.

Langston held the door for her to exit the elevator behind someone in a wheelchair. "Do you mind hanging around while I interview Gina if she is up to it? I need to ask her some questions while what happened is fresh on her mind. She is an excellent test case."

"No, I don't mind. I'd like to hear what she says too."

"Good. I've got to check her chart beforehand." Langston started down the long, tiled hallway, his boots making a thumping sound. "Then I'll meet you in her room."

Langston stopped at the nurses' station while Callee continued on to Gina's room. She knocked on the door then pushed it open. Sticking her head in, she said, "Hey there.'

"Hey. I knew you would be here early." Gina sat up in the bed as the sun began to shine through the windows of the room.

"Langston and I wanted to check on you before we went to work."

"I'm fine. You can stop worrying about me now."

"Gina, you could have really been hurt." That Callee knew too well. Head injuries she didn't take lightly.

Gina smoothed the sheet across her lap. "Yes, but I wasn't. I'm good. And I'm ready to go back to work."

"That will be up to your doctor, who thinks you need to take a few days off." Langston had entered without them hearing him.

"And my doctor needs to make more noise when he's coming in my room." Gina glared at him.

Langston appeared unaffected as he grinned at

her. "If I promise to be noisier, would you be willing to answer a few questions for my research?"

"Sure. What do you want to know?"

"I'll get to that. First I'd like to examine you." He adjusted the stethoscope hanging around his neck.

Callee sat on the edge of the plastic-covered chair on the other side of the room, well out of the way. She watched as Langston listened to Gina's heart and lungs.

He pulled out a penlight from his shirt's front pocket. "Gina, I want you to look just over my right shoulder. Focus on a spot. I'm going to check your eyes. Now, look up, down, left then right. Blink. Good. Is your vision blurry?"

All this time he spoke low and encouragingly to Gina. His bedside manner must be a large part of his success. Callee sat enthralled and she wasn't even his patient.

"No," Gina said.

"Good to hear. Now I would like to check your reflexes. Will you hang your feet off the side of the bed?"

Gina pushed away the covers and twisted until she was in the right position. Langston then went through the routine of tapping on her joints and watching her muscular reaction.

"Okay. Now I'd like to ask you a few questions." Langston let Gina settle under the covers once more. He took the other chair in the room, crossed one ankle over a knee and pulled out a small notepad from his pocket. "Now, tell me what you remember about the accident."

Gina went through how the horse wouldn't settle, that she knew he was raising his feet and the next thing she knew Langston was looking down at her at the hospital.

"When you woke, was your vision clear or blurry, or narrowed?"

"A little blurry."

Langston nodded. "I know I asked you to move your fingers, and you could, but did they hurt, hesitate, tingle?"

"None of that."

"Good. How about your head? Did it hurt then? Does it hurt now?"

"I have a little bit of a headache. Not bad, just an odd feeling that it's not right."

Langston jotted down a note. "I'd like to examine your head as well. All I'll do is run my fingers over your scalp. You tell me if any spot hurts while I check for bumps or indentions."

Over the next few minutes he slowly felt Gina's head. Callee sat amazed at how gentle and thorough he was.

At Gina's wince he looked at her face. "How bad does it hurt?"

"Not too bad."

"I'm going to order an MRI before you go

home." He stepped back and looked at her. "Your parents are here?"

Gina pursed her lips obviously not pleased with the turn of events. "Yes. They got in late last night."

"Good. I want someone with you for a few days or you stay in here."

Callee had no doubt from the firmness in his tone Langston wouldn't change his mind.

Fifteen minutes later she and Langston were on their way to Churchill Downs.

"What will you do with all that information you got from Gina?"

"I'll compare it to other people's I've interviewed. Right now, I'm particularly interested in the area of the head that the subjects have hit."

"Are you seeing signs of it being the same place?"

Langston grinned. "You are quick. Yes. And it would make sense to make helmets thicker and stronger there. In Gina's case even angling it farther down the neck. I will input my findings and suggestions then the engineers will go to work. It's a slow process but a rewarding one."

"So you've asked all those other people you interviewed the same questions."

"Mostly. Some are more in-depth because of what happened than others. Being kicked in the head by a horse is hard to prepare against. It's so unpredictable."

"What you are doing is more impressive than I first gave you credit for."

He chuckled. "I am glad I've gone up in your estimation."

Callee wouldn't tell him how much. She'd come to really like Langston. Too much.

"I appreciate you taking such good care of Gina."

He found her hand and squeezed it. "That's what I do."

Langston came to stand beside Callee at the rail every morning of the next week. It had become a ritual for him to bring her a coffee and meet her at the track. An occurrence he looked forward to. Oddly he'd never had a habit he shared with anyone, much less a woman.

Since their too hot kiss at her house, he'd kept his distance unless they were in public. He didn't trust himself alone with Callee. The more he learned about her, the more his desire for her had grown. Yet he shouldn't lead her to believe he might stay around. That wasn't in his DNA. It had been once, but he'd moved beyond that. Nothing about him was forever.

"Good mornin'." He handed her the cup of steaming brew.

"Hey." She smiled. "It's Derby Week. It's all hands on deck."

"That probably puts an end to the plans I had for this week."

"How's that?"

"I was going to the barns to see if I could interview some of the jockeys."

Callee's lips thinned. She shook her head. "Yeah, that probably is dead in the water. They will be too busy to talk."

"I have some other work I need to do anyway. Are you usually busy on these days?"

"It just depends."

A stable worker came running toward them. "Hey, Callee, come right now. Henry got his hand stuck in a trailer."

"Stuck in a trailer?" Langston looked from the young man to Callee.

"No telling what that means." Callee said. "Let me grab my bag. I'm on my way. Which barn?"

"Turner," the young man responded.

"Got it."

Langston grabbed his bag from the truck and climbed in the golf cart. Callee got in beside him. "You don't mind if I go too?"

"No, I can probably use your help."

Langston liked the fact Callee valued having him around. At first he wasn't sure she felt that way.

"Turner barn. Down on the right?"

"Yes. A couple of streets over and to the left. Barn seven."

Langston took off. Soon he pulled up to a group of people standing around a large horse trailer.

The trailer rattled with the stomping of horse's hooves against metal.

"So what's the problem?" Callee asked.

Langston looked around for someone hurt.

A man pointed. "Henry's inside."

"Is he hurt?" Langston asked in rapid Spanish. The man nodded.

"We need to get this horse out so we can get to him," Callee announced. "Let's get the horse settled down and out of here."

"He won't settle," one of the men close by said.

"Then get his trainer here with a restraint." Callee walked to the side of the trailer.

Langston joined her. She looked through the metal bars. Langston did as well. He could see a man standing in an awkward position.

"Henry, are you hurting?"

There was a groan and the man moved slightly.

"Are you bleeding?" Langston asked.

"Sí."

"Where?" Callee called.

"Arm. Broken maybe." The man forced the words out.

"Okay." She stepped back from the trailer. "It looks like he's hung on the latch that divides the trailer for two horses and is in the section with the horse."

Agitated, the horse shook the trailer again as it shifted positions.

"We need to get this temperamental horse out of here." She went to the side door and opened it, looking in at the wild-eyed animal.

Langston grabbed her arm. "What're you doing? Let these guys see about the horse. We don't need you getting hurt."

She glared over her shoulder. "I got this."

The horse jerked against the lead tied to the other side of the trailer.

Langston couldn't stand by and watch Callee get hurt. "I'm not letting you go in there."

Callee faced him, fury on her face. "I can handle it."

"Let one of these guys go in there." He nodded toward the men standing around.

"No. They can't touch a horse they don't work with."

Langston pointed. "What about the guy in there?"

"He works for the trainer."

Langston still didn't feel good about this. "Are you sure you know what you're doing?"

"I'm positive. You be prepared to go in and get the guy out while I see about the horse."

Langston shook his head. "I don't like it—"

Callee didn't wait for him to finish. "Stand back where the horse can't see you."

He shifted back two steps, but he refused to give

another inch. If she needed him, he'd know it. He would be able to see her.

"Hey, boy." Callee's voice had dropped to a soft sultry level.

The sound rippled over Langston's skin. Did she use the same tone when making love? He'd like to be on the receiving end of that attention. Apparently, the horse did as well. He looked at her. She reached out her hand.

"Easy, boy. I'm not here to hurt you."

Langston's chest tightened. He had to stand there and watch while someone he cared about walked into danger. He didn't normally stay around long enough for that to happen. Somehow Callee had gotten under her skin quickly.

"It's okay, boy." She continued to beseech the animal. Callee held the large horse's attention. She had Langston's as well. Slowly she walked to the horse with her hand outstretched. The animal lowered his head and jerked it up almost hitting Callee. In a reflex action, Langston stepped forward.

Callee spoke to him in a low tight voice that was a little more than a hiss through her teeth. "Don't move."

Langston had no doubt she spoke to him. He did as instructed, watching with his heart pounding. The hulking animal could run over Callee.

She continued to speak evenly to the horse. "All I want to do is help you."

The wildness ebbed from the horse's eyes. He lowered his head.

"Okay, boy, I'm going to reach out and touch you."

Langston questioned if she said that more for his sake than the horse's.

Callee touched the end of the horse's nose with the back of her hand. It shook its head, snorting. She waited patiently. After the horse settled she tried again. This time she slipped her hand under the halter. The horse jerked his head almost pulling Callee's feet off the floor, but she hung on.

Langston shifted.

"Not one step or sound."

This time Langston knew for a fact she spoke to him.

"Okay, boy. Let's go out and get some sun." She very carefully untied his lead and gave him a nudge forward. The horse resisted at first before it walked with her.

As she passed Langston, she said softly, "See about Henry."

Breathing a sigh of relief that Callee would be safe enough now that the horse was outside, he hurried into the trailer.

The man remained conscious. He still stood in a corner of the trailer with his arm in an awkward angle and above his head. As Langston approached, he could see his hand was caught in the latch between two sections of the trailer. "How did you manage to get into this situation?"

"The gate latch was stuck. I climbed up to kick it free. Then fell and my arm got hung."

"We'll have you out soon." Langston's attention went to the blood dripping on the wooden slat floor. He had to stop that flow right away.

"Henry, I'm Langston. A doctor. I need to see where this blood is coming from. It may hurt but I'll be as gentle as I can."

"Okay," he groaned.

Callee stepped into the trailer. "What have we got here?"

"Possible broken arm, bleeding from the biceps area, but not life threatening. What I need the most is a couple of guys to help me lift him up."

"I'll get them."

Two minutes later Callee, followed by two men, entered the trailer.

"I need one of y'all on the right side of me and the other on the left. Callee, I want you to call out what's happening with the arm and maneuver it out from between the bars as we lower him. On three everyone. One, two, three."

Langston grunted along with the other men as they lifted the awkwardly positioned Henry.

Callee called, "Hold. Let me work the arm out."

Langston watched with one eye as Callee carefully eased Henry's arm to freedom. "Okay, lower him." A moment went by. Callee said to Henry, "You're almost down."

"Put him on the floor," Langston told the two men.

Callee immediately placed her hand over where the blood flowed from Henry's upper arm. "I need my bag."

Langston pushed it to her then grabbed his own, going to his knees across from Callee.

"Let's get the bleeding under control then we can take him to the clinic." With one hand Callee dug into her bag for a pack of four-by-four gauze squares.

"Give it to me." Langston took the package and opened it, handing it back to her.

She applied the square to Henry's arm and pressed. "There's a roll of gauze in my bag."

"Here you go." Langston handed her a roll he'd pulled out of his bag.

Callee nodded. Evidently, she wasn't the only one who kept their bag prepared. "Okay, Henry, we're going to head up to the clinic and get you cleaned up." Callee stuffed things back into her bag. "We're going to help you outside. Do you think you can stand?"

"Sí."

"Good. Here we go." With Langston's help Callee got Henry to his feet. They walked with him between them out of the trailer. Someone had pulled the golf cart close.

She directed them. "Langston, if you'd drive, Henry and I'll sit in the back."

Langston took her bag and set it beside his in the front seat. Callee settled Henry and took her seat.

"Ready?" Langston asked.

"Go slowly."

"Got it." Langston took off with as small a jerk as possible, but Henry still moaned.

Callee told him, "We'll be at the clinic soon. I can give you something for the pain there."

Not soon enough for Henry, she was sure, Langston stopped in front of the clinic. Between the two of them they got him inside and settled in an exam room.

"You want me to get supplies or see about getting his shirt off?" Langston asked.

"Shirt." Callee stepped out in the hall for a moment to calm her temper. She had kept it contained while they worked with Henry, but it had started to bubble over. Langston had overstepped while she tried to get the horse out of the trailer.

Taking a deep breath, she went to the supply closet. When they were alone, she and Langston would have a few words. Her more than him. She returned to the examination room with her hands full.

Langston looked at her. His eyes widened a fraction in question. "You okay?"

"Yes. We'll talk about it later," she snapped.

His brows rose, but he returned his attention to their patient.

Despite the tension between them, they worked together to clean Henry's wound, which was nothing more than a large flesh wound. Then their focus went to his arm. After X-rays it was agreed that it wasn't broken just twisted badly. They placed Henry's arm in a sling.

"Henry, you're going to be on light duty for a few days. I want to see you back here in a week just for a check." Callee wrote him a prescription. "Take this for any pain."

"Thanks for helping me." He looked at her and then Langston. "I hear you're asking questions about people who have been hit in the head. I wasn't going to volunteer before today, but you're okay. I've been knocked out. I'll talk to you."

Langston put out his hand. "Thanks, Henry. I appreciate that. I'll come find you one day soon. Right now, you need to rest."

"I'll tell the others too." Henry smiled.

Langston returned it. "That would be a great help. Thanks."

"Carl's going to give you a ride back to the dorm." Callee led him out of the room toward the front door. It was time for her and Langston to talk. Her jaw tightened.

She returned to where Langston was straightening the room.

He faced her when she entered the room. "Is something bothering you?"

Callee glared at him. "Yes, it is."

"Having to do with me?" He wore an innocent look.

That fueled her anger. Langston had no idea what he had done. "Don't you ever try to stop me from doing my job again."

"What? When did I do that?" He looked perplexed.

"While I was trying to get to Henry."

"You mean when you were handling that enraged breast?"

"Yes. I knew what I was doing." She stomped to within arm's length of Langston. "I'm the lead person here. In a couple of weeks you'll be gone."

He bent to her eye level. "If you're ever in harm's way, I'll always say something or stop you."

She leaned toward him with her hands on her hips. "You have no say over me."

"I may not, but I can't and won't stand by while you do something dangerous. I didn't need two patients to care for."

"I knew what I was doing." She moved closer.

"I didn't care. I needed to know you'd be safe." His nose almost touched hers.

Callee glared. "Don't ever question or stop me when I'm trying to get to a patient ever again."

"Getting that horse out of the trailer wasn't your

job. And the horse was upset. You could've been hurt."

"It wasn't your place—"

Her words were cut off by Langston's mouth. His arms encircled her, crushing her to him from head to foot. She went up on her toes as he lifted her. Her hands held on to his shoulders while his tongue traced the seam of her mouth. On their own her lips opened to the sweet invader. Heat washed through her, pooling at her center. Her arms went around his neck and tightened as she took all he would offer.

She dipped her tongue inside his mouth. Langston groaned. One of his large hands traveled along her spine to cup her right butt cheek, bringing her securely in contact with his long thick manhood bulging between them.

In slow motion he lowered her. She had no choice but be aware of his desire.

He whispered in her ear. "Never doubt that when I fear for your well-being, I'll step in."

"But—"

He gave her a quick kiss. "There'll be no buts. It'll always be a fact. Now, do you have more excitement planned for today? Because I'd like to be prepared. Otherwise, I'm going out to see if I can conduct some interviews."

Callee rocked on her heels when he let her go and walked out the door.

* * *

Langston tugged at his collar behind the black bow tie of his tuxedo. He now remembered why it had been so long since he'd been to a formal affair. Oddly he hadn't flinched before agreeing to go with Callee.

After the scare she had put into him dealing with the horse, their argument and then that kiss that had him staying up at night, he'd been a mess for the last few days. His anticipation of this evening had only grown. At least tonight he would have Callee to himself with the safety net of them being among people. He could hold her in his arms while they danced. Maybe steal a kiss.

He walked toward Callee's front door. She had wanted to meet him at the ball, fearing she might be late because of last minute patients at the clinic. He'd insisted on picking her up. He had given her an irritated look then stated, "No, we agreed this was a date. I pick my dates up. They don't meet me places. Are you trying to get out of going with me?"

"I'm not," she had assured him. "I was just trying to make it easier on you."

"You don't need to worry about me."

He rang the doorbell and waited. Was she nervous about seeing him?

Langston's finger lay on the doorbell button to ring it again when Callee opened the door. His heart did a flip-flop and burst into a fast gallop at the sight of her. She was gorgeous. She'd been pretty before but with her hair pulled back in a wild little bun, her eyes made up to accent their size and the lines of her dress hugging her curves she was breathtaking.

In slow motion she studied him from the top of his head to the tips of his shiny black shoes pinching his feet. A slow smile came to her lips. "No boots."

Heat warmed him at her appraisal. He grinned. "I left my dress boots in Texas."

Their gazes met.

He said, "You have to be the most gorgeous thing I've ever seen."

"Thank you. You look quite dashing yourself."

"There's no way you won't be the most beautiful woman at the ball. I'll be proud to have you on my arm."

She turned away to gather her purse. "You keep that kind of talk up, and I might start to believe you."

As she joined him, he said, "You should because it's true. Come, your chariot awaits." He offered her his arm and escorted her along the sidewalk.

The driver hopped out of the car, came around and opened the back passenger door for them.

"You got a driver for tonight," Callee said in awe.

"I thought I'd enjoy sitting in the back with you.

I didn't think my truck was what we needed to roll up in."

"You didn't have to do this, but I have to admit it's wonderful." Pleasure filled her voice.

Langston helped her into the car then climbed in beside her. She giggled when he had to work his long legs into the space.

"Are you laughing at me?"

"No, never." But her eyes twinkled with mischief.

He grinned. At least she was releasing some of her nervous energy.

Soon they were rolling away from the curb and toward downtown Louisville.

"By the way. I like your hair. I hadn't expected that hairdo."

Callee touched her bun. "Yeah, it was Gina's idea. She said you've been checking on her every day."

"I want to make sure she's recovering well."

"And get a few study notes." She watched him.

"That too but mostly making sure she doesn't have any residual problems."

Callee shifted into the seat, getting comfortable. "She seems like her old self, but she still hasn't returned to work."

"I'm glad to know you haven't noticed anything amiss. The ones closest usually see it first."

"Some people don't." Sadness washed over her face. The smile that had been there faded.

Langston wished he hadn't said anything. He was confident her thoughts had gone straight to her old boyfriend. He took her hand. "Nothing but fun thoughts tonight. You're on a date with me, and I want you to have a good time. Tell me about the ball."

"All the bigwigs of Churchill Downs will be there, including my boss. But you know him. Also many of the horse owners and some of the famous trainers attend. This is the first time I've ever been. I'm not sure why I was invited."

"Don't sell yourself short. You're an important part of keeping things going on the backside."

"Maybe so but these people are out of my league."

It was more like she was out of theirs. Callee had built a pig puddle of guilt around her she couldn't see past to the amazing person beyond. "Looking like you do, they're nowhere near your league."

"You are too kind."

"I tell the truth." He took her hand and squeezed it then released it.

The closer they came to downtown Louisville the more Callee clasped and unclasped her hands. She was afraid. Langston had been convinced she feared nothing. "Callee, settle down. There's no reason to be so nervous."

She looked at him with tight lips. "I bet you do this sort of thing all the time."

More often than he liked but not regularly. "I don't."

"Yeah, but I bet when you do go it's by choice, rather than feeling you have to." She looked out the window as if judging whether to hop out at the next light or not.

"That part might be true."

"These are your kind of people not mine. I don't even know what they're talking about half the time. I'm just a physician assistant who happens to work at the clinic."

"You're lovely and intelligent, and you have nothing to worry about. They're just people like you and me."

She studied him a moment. "Nobody's like you." She ran her hand down his lapel. "You are very handsome."

"Thank you. I like hearing that from you."

Their driver pulled into the line behind the other cars waiting to unload in front of the modern large hotel in downtown Louisville. Their turn came. Langston slipped out of the car and offered Callee his hand. She didn't hesitate to place hers in his. He helped her out.

He shouldn't be so taken by a woman. Or even care about her feelings to the point he would protect her. Yet Callee had him doing just that against his better judgment. "Remember tonight we're just a couple on a date. We'll just pretend no one else is around and enjoy each other."

She smiled. One that reached her eyes. "That I can do."

CHAPTER SIX

CALLEE HADN'T BEEN able to help being jittery with excitement during the past week. She had tried to pretend it was everything to do with Derby Week and nothing to do with going to the ball with Langston. But she knew better. She was looking forward to spending time with him. If he hadn't agreed to go with her she probably would have found an excuse not to attend. Balls weren't her type of thing. Give her a barn, a horse and she was happy.

Derby Week was always an exhilarating time, but this year it was over the top. As the time for the ball drew near, she became thankful for the steady stream of patients to keep her mind settled. If left with too much time to think, she would turn into a bundle of nerves.

She couldn't remember the last time she had been so concerned about her looks. Working around the backside, what she wore mattered little as long as it was functional. Regardless, the last thing she wanted was to embarrass herself or Langston.

One evening she'd managed to find a dress. Fortunately, she'd found one quickly. A dusky rose color with simple lines and a flowing skirt. It was an extravagant expense on her income, but the look on Langston's face had made it worth it.

She had been too busy to take time off to have her hair done. So Gina had insisted that Callee go to her house and let her do it. Callee had relented, even agreeing to something modern yet traditional. Later she had spent extra time on her makeup, something she rarely wore.

She was glad she had after seeing Langston's expression. He looked so handsome in his black tux with the white pleats across his chest and the black skinny bow tie. The shiny black strip running along his slacks side seam make his legs appear longer. Everything about Langston made her heart race. Callee thought she might melt right there in front of him when she had seen him.

When he'd complimented her, she'd felt it all the way to her toes. The man had a way of making her feel beautiful. She couldn't help but appreciate the possessiveness that filled his voice. It had been so long since someone claimed her as theirs. She liked the sound of it. She would have the best-looking person in the room as her date.

Tonight, she would forget the past and enjoy.

Langston ushered her into the revolving door of the hotel. Stepping out, she put her hands under her wrap and ran them over the silky material of her dress.

He took her hand and whispered close to her ear, "You look beautiful. Smile. No scowling tonight."

"I'm not scowling."

"Sometimes you do." He grinned.

"Only when you're making me really mad."

They continued down the hall. "Tonight the idea is for you to be really happy. Let's go enjoy. I'm looking forward to dancing with you."

She hesitated. Dance. "I don't dance."

"I hope you will with me. Don't worry, I'll take care of you." That was the second time he had said that. Something about his tone made her believe he would be there for her as he promised. She'd never considered herself the type of person who needed someone to take care of her, yet she liked the idea of being under Langston's watchful eyes.

They strolled down the long corridor with other couples. Callee looked at each man, but none of them measured up to Langston's strong presence. She shook herself mentally. Langston had her head tangled up with emotions.

She could hear the sounds of a party not far away. After showing their invitation, they entered the ballroom to the soft sound of the band and the chattering of people. A number of them were in groups.

Langston took her elbow. "Let's see if we can find a place to sit."

They circled around the room until they found

available seats at a table where only one other couple sat. Langston made the introductions.

A waiter came around to ask if they would like to have a drink. He carried highball glasses with a finger of dark liquid in them. There were also silver tumblers with a mint sprig sticking out of the top. Langston accepted bourbon in the highball glass.

He looked at her. "Don't worry. I won't overindulge."

Callee's chest tightened. "I know you think I'm being silly."

"No, I think you had a traumatic experience that you're having a difficult time getting beyond. We all can say that on some level."

"Thanks. Did you know that a mint julep is the traditional drink of the Kentucky Derby?"

"I'm not surprised since this state is the bourbon capital of the world."

She relaxed. "Maybe I could have one mint julep. It has been a long time."

"You don't have to do that to make me happy."

"I trust you to be responsible. Therefore, I should trust myself as well. I know I shouldn't be such a prude about it. But it scares me." She suddenly wanted to let go of the past. To accept she couldn't have done any more for Joe than she had. If only she could believe that.

"You don't owe me any explanations. I like you just the way you are."

Her heart opened to him. "Thank you for that."

Langston took a swallow of his drink. "I'm not in this area often, so it's hard for me to pass up fine bourbon especially since so much of it is made here."

The waiter made another trip around. This time Callee accepted a mint julep.

Langston raised his glass and she tapped hers against his.

She took a sip. "I forgot that it was more lemonade with a lot of crushed ice than bourbon."

"Good?" Langston watched her.

She smiled. "Good."

"Tell me what will happen tomorrow." He leaned in closer.

Would he kiss her? When he didn't she said, "Tomorrow is the Kentucky Oaks race. It's for the three-year-old fillies. There will be thirteen races. Many of the women spectators, and the men too, wear pink to bring awareness to breast cancer and ovarian cancer. Everyone comes as well-dressed for tomorrow's races as they will be on Saturday. The Oaks race is the eleventh one of the day. A blanket of pink lilies is presented to the winner."

"Will we get to see any of this?" He took a sip of his drink.

"Nope. All that happens on the other side of the track at the grandstands."

"Really? None of it?"

"I usually catch some of the races on the monitor in the clinic waiting room. What we do see is some of the horses headed for their race. Saturday is Derby Day, and there are fourteen races. For the people attending, it's all about the three-year-old males running. The winning horse receives a blanket of red roses. The men and the women are well-dressed. Many of the women wear the most amazing hats. People watching is a real thing."

"Except you are stuck in the clinic." He pursed his lips.

She shrugged. "It's my job."

"I know but wouldn't it be nice to attend one race?"

"It would." She had another sip of her drink. "I had forgotten how good one of these is."

"Watching the races on TV doesn't sound like it's the same as being there."

"It isn't, but you can still feel the excitement in the backside. The horses are coming and going for their run in the greatest two minutes in sports. They are calmly walking and fifteen minutes later they running as if for their life. They barrel around the track with the jockey urging them on. How can you not find a thrill in that?"

"I can see your point." Langston smiled. "It does sound exciting."

"Horse racing is an extremely expensive sport. It requires a major investment. People to train the horse, care for it, vet bills, barn costs and it goes on and on. All just for that moment their horse crosses the finish line first. To win the Triple Crown is almost impossible."

He raised his brows. "Triple Crown?"

"Are you sure you don't know all this?"

"Maybe I do, maybe I don't. Either way I enjoy listening to you. You get very animated about the subject."

She studied his handsome features and recognized the twinkle in his eyes. "Are you making fun of me?"

"I would never do that." He grinned. One that gave her a bird in flight feeling in her middle. "So what's the Triple Crown?"

"It's when the horse wins the Kentucky Derby, Preakness Stakes and the Belmont Stakes. All in the same year. If they do that, their racing career is over."

Concern filled his voice. "At three years old?"

"Yep." She grinned. "They get a new job. They put them out to stud."

He leaned close, giving her a wolfish grin. "Now that's a career I could get behind."

Her center tingled. She bet he would be good at it too. "I thought you might."

"Did you go to the Derby when you were growing up?"

"No, that was too adult an event. My parents felt like the liquor was too free-flowing and people sometimes behaved badly. Plus it is expensive to get tickets. We did watch it on TV like some people watch the Super Bowl."

The band began playing again. Langston stood and offered his hand. "Would you care to dance with me?"

Callee hesitated a moment. She had little experience with dancing, but she couldn't pass up a chance on being in Langston's arms. Taking his hand she said, "I will, but it needs to be slow and easy and not too many fancy steps."

"I promise to take care of you."

She didn't doubt he meant it. Langston was the type of man who took care of those he cared about.

He held her hand as they walked to the dance floor. There he wrapped an arm around her, bringing her close. He was so much taller than Callee, but her high heels helped. Her head almost reached his shoulder. They slowly moved around the floor along with the other dancers. It was wonderful, dazzling and disturbing at the same time. She enjoyed being in Langston's arms too much.

She pressed her cheek against his chest. He tightened his arms. They swayed to the music. She relaxed listening to the steady reassuring beat of Langston's heart. Was it wrong to wish it could last forever?

Langston had not prepared to relish holding Callee as much as he did. It had been too long since he'd last had her in his arms. It felt so right having her next to him. He enjoyed it more than he should have. Despite their height difference they fit. He led her around the dance floor with little effort, pressing her close.

Callee was a strong, vibrant woman who knew her own mind, yet she carried insecurities. Her past dictated her future. The accident with her college boyfriend had frozen her in time. An irrational guilt lay heavy on her. Just seeing him pick up a drink sent her spinning into what could happen.

Her small hand drifted down the breast of his jacket, pushing all other thoughts but of touching her from his mind. She smiled and his middle constricted.

He kissed the top of her head. "You take my breath away."

Their dancing turned from less about moving around the floor to more about touching each other. He could get used to this. Too easily. He had his next job to think about. A long-distance relationship rarely worked out. He knew from experience. It wouldn't be fair for Callee to always be waiting on him to return. If she did. Emily hadn't. Or had he been unrealistic to think she would? But Callee was different. Stronger, more confident in her abilities. Still, she deserved better than to spend her days waiting on him. Could he leave her alone? She pulled at him just as gravity pulled at the earth. To break away might send him spinning into nothingness. The music ended. They looked at the band.

A man stepped to the microphone and said, "Dinner is served." Maybe it was just as well they had to take a break. He might have touched her more freely, and she wouldn't want her bosses to notice.

They lined up with the others at the buffet. Callee faced the table. "This is unreal. Look at that ice sculpture of horses racing. And all this food. I'm out of my league."

He leaned close and said for her only, "You are far beyond everyone here."

Her soft smile grabbed his heart and squeezed. They filled their plates, returning to their table. By this time two more couples had joined them. During their meal, they had a lively discussion about past Derby Weekends and the number of times they had experienced it. They all poked fun at him because he'd never attended.

Callee squeezed his knee then stepped in to defend him. "I've lived within two hours of here all my life and I've never sat in the grandstands before."

The eyes of the other couples widened in disbelief. "Really?"

Langston sat straighter having her support. That was something he could get used to.

With dinner completed they returned to the

dance floor. Callee said, "I hope they weren't too hard on you back there."

He lifted a shoulder. "I'm pretty thick-skinned, but it was nice to have you defend me. I found it very sexy."

Callee hesitated a beat and Langston stepped on her foot. He looked at her with concern. "I'm sorry. Is your foot, okay?"

"My fault. I just saw Dr. Bishop."

Langston recognized the man as being her boss. He was also the person who Langston had discussed his project with four weeks ago.

"I should speak to him so he'll know I attended." She didn't sound like she really wanted to, but he guided her off the dance floor. As they approached the older gentleman, his gray eyebrows rose. He looked between the two of them, then at Langston's hand resting at her waist.

"Hi, Dr. Bishop. I wanted to say thank you for the invitation to the ball."

"I'm glad you could attend. And bring Dr. Watts with you. I realize this is a busy time for you with very little chance to appreciate the Derby festivities."

Langston shook hands with the older man. "You're right, she doesn't take much time for herself."

Dr. Bishop studied him a moment. "I understand you two make a good team. We hear things from the backside all the way to the front office."

"We have had a couple of interesting cases since Langston arrived, but things will settle down again after the Derby. He's been a lot of help." She looked at Langston and smiled.

"I hope you've had a chance to do your research as well."

"I have. I've gotten a lot of excellent data," Langston assured him.

He nodded. "Good to hear."

Two overweight gentlemen with highball glasses in their hands joined them.

"Bob," one said to Dr. Bishop, "are these the two people you were telling us about?"

"It is." Dr. Bishop made the introductions of Dr. Mitchell, and Mr. Sorensen, the CEO at Churchill Downs.

"Dr. Watts, your reputation precedes you. Nice to meet you," Dr. Mitchell said, shaking Langston's hand, followed by Mr. Sorensen.

Langston turned to Callee. "This is Callee Dobson. She's the brilliant PA who runs the clinic." He sensed more than saw her anxiety at the arrival of the two men.

"It's a pleasure to meet you, Mr. Sorensen. I've heard a lot about you. Dr. Mitchell, it's a pleasure to meet you as well."

Dr. Mitchell said, "Aw, just the person I was hoping to speak to. I hear you're almost as good with horses as caring for people. I'm looking at starting a new program that works with the jockeys and horses. You'd care for the jockeys but also study their interactions with the horses. I need people who understand both groups. It's a rare person who has skills and qualifications on the human side and an understanding and appreciation of horses too. I heard about how you handled the situation with the man who had been caught in the horse trailer."

Callee raised her chin. "Thank you, sir. My father is a veterinarian."

Dr. Mitchell said, "I'd like you to consider coming to work with me. Possibly progress to the head of the program in a couple of years. Would you consider it?"

Callee glanced at Dr. Bishop. He said, "You'd go with my blessing. We already discussed your qualifications. I'd hate to see you go, but you'd have my wholehearted support if you did. Apparently, many of your talents are wasted with us."

Callee shifted. "Dr. Mitchell, I don't know what to say. I'm happy where I am."

"I can appreciate that, but please think about what I've said. If you change your mind, Dr. Bishop knows how to get in touch with me."

Mr. Sorensen said, "Callee, I'd like to offer my thanks for your quick and sure actions regarding the situation with the horse with the flu. If it hadn't been for your actions, the Derby might not be running this year. If there is ever anything you need, please let me know."

"Thank you, sir, but I'm sure somebody else would have recognized it…"

The older man said, "They may have, but it also might have been too late."

"I'm glad I was there at the time," Callee said. A woman with a neck encircled by jewels called Mr. Sorensen's name and waved him toward her. He said his goodbyes and left. The other two men did as well. Langston gave her a gentle squeeze. "You must be proud of yourself. That was a nice job offer. I'm glad for you. It's well deserved."

Callee's eyes filled with shadows. "I haven't thought about another job."

"It would give you a chance to work with people and their medical needs along with using your practical experience from working with horses and your father. You are in the unique position of understanding the horse and rider. It would be the best of both worlds. Perfect for you."

"It would but my place is at the clinic." She looked overwhelmed.

Not wanting to upset Callee tonight, Langston kept his opinion of how she hid at the clinic because she felt guilty about what happen to her boyfriend. That she hadn't been able to save his life. Mentioning it would only start an argument. Something he wasn't doing this evening. "All I'll say about it now is you have so much to offer any place you work."

"Thank you. That's a nice thing to say." That wiped the shadows from her eyes.

"It's easy to say nice things to you. You're nice. Would you like to have a few more dances then slip out of here?"

He tightened his hold, bringing her against him for a second.

"That sounds good to me. I have to be at the clinic early."

"In that case I'll need to be there too." He escorted her to the dance floor and with a flourish brought her into his arms.

Callee giggled and smiled at him. This dreamy feeling must be what heaven felt like. She stepped closer. The arm at her waist tightened. Langston had started to become part of what made her happy. They danced to a fast song, then he brought her to him again for the slower one. He held her tight, her hips cradled against him. His hand lay low on the curve of her back. Hot heat of want filled her. His body brushed hers with his every movement. The song ended. Langston whispered, "Let's get out of here."

"I'm ready." For more than leaving the party. She was ready to have Langston to herself. They returned to their table and said their goodbyes. Langston helped her with her wrap. His hands caressed her shoulders for a moment as he smoothed the material into place. Taking her hand, he walked toward the door matching his pace to hers, yet there was a determination to his movements.

She tightened her hand around his. "Is there some hurry I don't know about?"

"I'm sorry, sweetheart." He stopped giving her a look of concern. "I didn't mean to drag you along. I'm just anxious to kiss you."

Her heart revved like a motor. "Oh. Then let's go."

His lips formed a vivid smile. Soon they were climbing in the back seat of the car. It had hardly moved off when Langston took her in his arms. His kiss made her blood heat and speed throughout her body. Callee clung to him as he ravaged her mouth. She returned his need. Making a half turn, she faced him. Her fingers plowed through his hair as she held his head to hers.

His hand ran up her leg bringing her dress with it. She moaned. His lips released hers. She blinked coming out of the Langston created daze. He nipped at her earlobe. "Not here. Soon." Horrified she had come close to letting him undress her in the back seat of a car with another man not feet away. She scooted away and straightened her dress.

Langston grinned and leaned in close, giving her a light kiss. "Don't go too far." He gave her hand a tug, encouraging her to move closer. She did so, leaning her head on the upper part of his arm. They didn't say much as they finished the ride. Finally the driver pulled alongside the curb in front of her house.

After climbing out, Langston then helped her. He pulled her hand through his arm and rested his hand over that one. They strolled to the front door. Taking her keys, he opened the door.

Was she just going to let him go? She didn't want that. "Would you like to come in for a cup of coffee?"

He looked at her for a long moment. "Callee, if I come in it won't be for a cup of coffee."

Unable to stop herself she said, "I don't want a cup of coffee either."

"You need to be sure."

With complete confidence she said, "I'm sure."

CHAPTER SEVEN

CALLEE LEFT THE door open while Langston returned to speak to the driver. She dropped her purse and wrap on a living room chair, then kicked off her shoes beside it as she passed. She stood in the kitchen filling the coffeepot with water when she heard the door close. She called, "I'm in here."

She felt the moment Langston entered the room and faced him. "I thought you might change your mind."

Langston removed his suit jacket and hung it on a chair at the table. He watched her a moment with predatory eyes before walking toward her. He stopped in front of Callee, leaving her plenty of room to step around him. "I haven't changed my mind. About coffee. I'm more interested in this."

He kissed her but never placed his hands on her. She fisted his shirt in her hands to steady herself against the onslaught of emotions flooding her. Langston had her quivering all over.

She'd questioned her boldness of asking him to stay, but there was only so much time left before Langston would be gone. She'd decided the moment he kissed her in the car she wanted one night to remember. She had never felt like this about another man. It had been so long since she'd let herself care about someone at this level. She had a difficult time letting go of the barriers she'd created to protect herself. Langston had slowly pulled that wall down brick by brick, kiss by kiss.

He backed her to the counter away from the coffee maker. Placed his hands against the counter, boxing her in yet she didn't feel threatened. She was right where she wanted to be. Callee reached her hands around his neck, playing with the silky hair at his nape.

His lips met hers with a demand that heated her core. Their tongues danced and mated.

He lifted her onto the counter then returned to kissing her neck. His fingers found the hem of her dress. His hands branded the skin of her calves before he ran them along the outside of her legs, pushing the material higher to gather across her thighs. He stepped between her legs.

Her hands ran across the ridge of his shoulder kneading his taut muscles. He lifted her hips. Tugging on her dress, she bunched it around her waist.

Langston stepped closer as he continued to caress the outside of her legs. He kissed her shoulder then found the dip below her neck. Her nipples hardened, pushing against the fabric of her dress.

Callee murmured her pleasure. Her head lolled back against the cabinet door. She closed her eyes while she soaked in Langston's heated desire.

"You feel so good." His fingers feather-brushed

each vertebra as he lowered the dress's zipper down her back to her hips. With each touch the throbbing at her center grew stronger. Her breathing slowed, held with anticipation.

Langston hooked a finger beneath the shoulder strap of her dress and pushed it down inch by inch. He kissed her neck, to her shoulder then across and back before he moved to the hollow of her neck again. There the tip of his tongue flicked out to taste her.

She squirmed. He held her secure on the counter. His hands brushed the straps to her elbows revealing her breasts. She moved to cover herself, but Langston stopped her.

"Such beauty should never be covered."

Callee heated inside and outside as Langston looked at her. Using his lips, he touched the top curve of a breast and moved down. His tongue circled her nipple. Pulling away in a gradual motion, he gave her a gentle tug. "So sweet. So responsive."

Langston continued to explore and tease her breasts. Her center ached while her breaths turned heavy, and short.

She wanted Langston. All of him. Desperately.

He stepped back, lifting her breasts. "Watch me, Callee. See how I adore you."

Doing as he demanded, she raised her head and saw him lift her breasts as if testing their weight. His tongue darted out to taste a nipple before he sucked and then did the same to the other.

Callee's center contracted. She squirmed. She held his mouth to her while he teased, tortured and tested her reaction. His tongue twirled around her nipple, tugging. She savored the feeling along with his attention. Her breasts grew heavier, her center wet.

His gaze met hers. "You're everything I dreamed you'd be."

She blinked. He'd been dreaming of her. Callee cupped his cheeks and brought his mouth to hers, kissing him deeply.

His hands ran up her legs to clasp her hips, slid up her butt. He lifted her to the edge of the counter. His manhood pressed into her center. She flexed into him.

"Sweetheart, too much of that and it'll all be over too soon." Desire had darkened his blue eyes to storm cloud gray.

Holding her gaze, he let his finger trace the top of her panty line causing her middle to quiver. Her fingertips bit into his shoulders as his finger slipped under the elastic to brush between her legs. Her center beat like a drum. Langston's look bore into hers. He continued to hold her look as his finger slid between her legs. Callee widened her legs involuntarily to give him better advantage.

Langston growled. "I need to touch you. Lift your hips."

She didn't hesitate. Pressing her palms against the counter, she lifted her hips.

Seconds later Langston had stripped off her underwear. He dropped them to the floor without a backward glance. His look captured hers. He stepped between her legs once more. His hands lay on her thighs.

Callee's breathing grew faster in anticipation. Her hands gripped his biceps. His thumbs unhurriedly stroked the sensitive skin between her legs, moving closer to where her body begged for his touch. Still his eyes didn't waver.

"Tell me what you want?"

Could she?

"Tell me." His eyes demanded. His tone demanded. His hands gave her thighs a gentle squeeze.

"Touch me." The words were little more than a whisper.

The pad of his thumbs swept her center.

She shuddered.

"I love how you react to my touch." His mouth found hers in a hot, wet, sensual kiss.

His finger entered her. Callee's body flexed, clasped around him. Her legs widened giving Langston all the space she could. His touch had her holding on to him to keep from spinning off. She wanted more. Ached for it.

Langston removed his finger.

She moaned her disappointment.

His tongue simulated the same as his finger reentering her, moving faster.

A tightness grew, intensified, spun and built on

itself until it exploded. She threw her head back and shook as she wailed her gratification. Thrown into a world she'd not experienced before, she hung there in the bliss and floated back to reality. Panting, her head fell forward to rest on Langston's shoulder. She shivered.

Langston's arms circled her, pulling her close. "Bedroom."

"End of the hall."

With an arm around her waist and the other behind her knees, he lifted her against his chest.

Callee held on to Langston's neck as he worked his way down the hall to the open door at the end. Taking three long steps, he stood beside the bed. He gently laid her in the center. She held her dress over her chest.

"I don't know why you're clutching that dress over those beautiful pieces of womanhood when I was feasting on them a few minutes ago." He bent a knee and leaned over her.

She stopped him with a hand on his chest. "Maybe because I expect equal time."

He grinned. "Not a problem."

Callee watched with rapt attention, not missing a movement of Langston undressing. His long nimble fingers, which she knew so well, now released each button from its hole in rapid succession on his shirt. Callee appreciated the slow sexy reveal of Langston's chest. Unlike when they were in the stall, she got to enjoy the muscles flexing and contracting across his chest as he worked. Finished with the buttons, he shrugged out of the shirt and let it drop to the floor.

He sat on the edge of the bed and removed his shoes.

She took advantage of the opportunity to run her hands over his back valuing the muscle and strength there. She kissed his shoulders and nape. Her arms encircled his neck. She pressed her breasts against his back as her hands explored his chest, enjoyed the dusting of hair there.

"You keep this up and I might undress for you again." He turned to kiss her.

"I would enjoy that." She kissed across his shoulder.

Langston groaned. "Mmm. I like that."

She nipped the top of his shoulder.

Langston jerked to his feet and shucked his pants. His black biking shorts quickly followed.

Callee admired his trim waist, firm butt and steady thighs. The man was as gorgeous from the back as he was from the front. She enjoyed the private showing.

Langston reached for his pants and pulled out his wallet, removing a couple of packages of protection. He placed them on the bedside table. Turning to her, he asked, "May I help you remove your dress?"

Callee smiled. So formal sounding. Langston stood there in all his magnificent glory. His manhood tall and thick. "I was wrong about your truck."

"What?" His eyes held confusion.

"In your case I was wrong about the size of your truck being a reflection of your inadequacies."

Langston gave her a wolfish grinned. "Compliment taken."

He reached for the hem of her dress. "Okay?"

"Yes." She let go of her dress as he tugged it over her head, slowly revealing her legs, her stomach and with a shoosh of material, all of her.

Langston dropped the dress in a rose-color pile beside his formal clothes with no regard for care. His focus remained on her. His eyes burned with need. "Honey, I desire you like I have no other."

Callee felt the same. Want made her body tense, jittery and hot. She watched in fascination as he opened a package and rolled on the protection.

Langston came down beside her, bringing her close. He nuzzled her neck. His knee moved between her legs. Callee gave no resistance. She wanted this. Running a hand to her breasts, he fondled them. She enjoyed the feel of being in his large, gentle hands. Her nipples rose to greet him. He accepted the call, giving them both equal attention with his mouth. Sliding over Callee, he settled between her legs. His tip lay just outside her entrance, waiting.

She raised her knees cradling him in her heat and dampness.

Langston met and held her gaze. "You're sure about this? I want no regrets in the morning."

"I've never been surer. I want you inside me," Callee said with confidence she felt down into her soul.

His lips found hers.

Her heartbeat increased in anticipation. Blood rushed to her center.

Langston rose on his hands. Slowly, exquisitely so, he entered her, settled deep. He didn't move as if he were savoring the experience. His jaw tightened. He pulled away and pushed in once again then increased the rhythm.

Callee flexed to meet him. He increased the tempo. She squirmed, begging for more. She clutched at Langston, holding him. He didn't slow. The sensation built, swirled, curled, expanded, climbed higher and crashed.

He continued to plunge into her.

"Langston…" she crooned as she floated to an ecstasy she had never known. She returned to earth shattered and weak, and complete.

Renewing his efforts, Langston drove into her. Callee wrapped her arms around him. He stiffened. With eyes shut, he made long strokes. With a groan that sounded forced from him, he found release, shuttered and collapsed.

His weight pressed her into the mattress. Callee ran her hands over his back, loving the feel of the strong man beneath her fingers. She liked touching him. So much.

Just before she would have to complain about his weight he rolled to her side. Langston's hands encircled her waist and pulled her close. He hauled the edge of the bedspread over them.

Callee closed her eyes and snuggled against his warmth.

He murmured, "I like it when you scream my name."

Callee reached for the offending alarm clock and shut it off. It couldn't be time to get up.

She wiggled into the warmth at her back. Hadn't she just gone to sleep?

A firm long arm wrapped around her waist and pulled her back against a sturdy chest. Mmm… Langston.

His mouth nuzzled her neck. One of his hands covered her bare breast. "Let's chuck it all and stay here."

That sleep-roughed voice made her skin ripple, sending heat to her core. "People who go from one part of the country to the next don't have to worry about showing up for work. Those of us who go in regularly do. It's Derby Weekend. The busiest we have. I have to work."

"You had a job offer last night," he murmured against the top of her head.

An offer she hadn't much time to think about

that. All she had been concerned with was Langston and his touch. She smiled. It had felt delicious last night just as it did now.

Langston's hand slipped to the V of her legs. Her center throbbed. "We don't have time."

He nipped at her ear. "We can save time by showering together."

Would she ever get enough of this man?

She rolled to face him. His lips found hers. Her arms went around his neck. Langston rolled to his back. Her legs straddled his hips. His hands rested at her hips. She leaned down to kiss him. He lifted her so his manhood easily slipped inside her. She settled on him. This she could get used to having all the time.

But she dared not. Yet she would enjoy it while it lasted.

Half an hour later Callee lay basking in the feeling of being well loved. Her entire body felt like warm putty Langston had played with. She glanced at the clock and despite her desire to remain where she lay, she sat straight up. "I've got to get going. You're a bad influence."

"You can't blame me. You were in control this morning."

She had been. And loved it. Langston was a generous lover. "You complaining?"

"Hell, no." He grinned as if he'd just won the Derby.

"I'm going to get a quick shower, then I'm headed

out. If you want a ride, you'd better be thinking about getting out of that bed." She snatched jeans out of the closet and found a T-shirt in the chest of drawers. "If you want to call a service to pick you up, you're welcome to stay. I'll see you at the clinic later."

"I definitely need to go by my place. I don't think showing up in my tux is a good idea."

"You'd be the best dressed doctor there today."

"Yeah, but I miss my boots."

She grinned. "And you might need that big red truck."

He chuckled, rose and stalked toward her. "Are you besmirching my manhood again?"

She gave him a wicked look then dashed into the bathroom. "What if I am?"

"Then I'll need to prove you wrong. Again."

Callee giggled as she stepped under the warm spray of the shower. The morning after should have been uncomfortable but with Langston it all seemed so natural, easy.

"Don't hog the water." Langston gave her a little pop on the butt and stepped in with her. "I'll wash you if you'll wash me."

"I don't think this is a good idea."

"Come on, Callee. Where is that adventurous spirit of yours?" He took her in his arms.

Bathing with a man wasn't something she had done. She and Joe had been kids. Langston was a man with different wants and needs. She couldn't help but touch his water-slicked body.

Langston growled. "You keep that up and we'll be having our own race. To the bed."

Only five minutes late, Callee pulled into her parking spot. There were many more vehicles in the area than usual, as it was Kentucky Oaks day. The place was teaming with people and horses.

There would be no breeze that morning, so she headed straight to the clinic.

Two people were already standing outside the clinic door waiting on her. And it wasn't even daylight yet. The grandstands across the track had no one in them yet. They would fill up later that morning. Right now, all the activity was on her side of the track.

Unlocking the door, she let her patients inside. She had seen one of them before. The woman had a simple cut on her hand. Even that had to be taken care of when working around animals. An infection could so easily set in. Callee cleaned and bandaged it, writing out instructions to wear a glove and come back to see her in three days.

Fifteen minutes later Langston arrived. She heard him speaking to Carl and then to the man waiting. At the sound of footsteps, she looked away from her patient to see Langston leading the man to an exam room. She liked having his help and support. Liked having him around far more than she should.

They sent their patients out as the same time.

"Callee, I need to ask you about a file in your office." Langston started down the hall.

"I need to clean up the room then I'll be along."

Langston gave her a pointed look then strolled on.

Her brows drew together. What was that about? Was he regretting their night together already? She quickly put things in the exam room away and hurried to her office. "What's up?"

Langston stood and closed the door behind her. "I missed you."

"You just saw me."

"Yeah, but I didn't get a kiss."

She liked silly, befuddled Langston. The day they met she'd thought him a stuffed shirt. He had an air of superiority. Then, he started to let his hair down. She had a chance to see the man beneath.

"Then we need to fix that." Feeling a little off center herself, her hands went behind his head and pulled his lips down to hers. She gave him a kiss that had them both hot.

They broke contact. Langston rested his forehead against hers. "You keep kissing me like that, and I'm not gonna be able to see patients."

"Then you better watch out."

Langston concluded he'd made a mistake of a lifetime. But no way would he have done anything different. He'd let himself become involved with Callee. She'd started to really matter in his life. His heart moved closer to becoming involved. He cared for Callee more than he should for a man leaving town in a few weeks.

He'd never felt like this before. With anyone. Not even Emily. He wanted to run, but then he didn't. What made it worse was he didn't want to share these emotions with anyone but Callee. Yet he couldn't stay. Would she consider going with him? He had a job to do. One that was important and mattered.

He couldn't call what he had in Texas a home. He was rarely there. It was more like an expensive storage room or glorified hotel. He dropped things off and then left again. Callee's place was a home. It looked and felt like who she was. It had life in it. What did he expect? For her to leave that to follow him around the world?

Callee loved what she was doing. The people she worked with. Knew them, shared her life so much that she didn't even want to consider taking a different job, one that was tailor-made made for her.

He had no one he could call a best friend. Not since Mark. Hadn't he found that again here at Churchill Downs? People spoke to him when he went by. Came up to him to ask questions. Had accepted him as part of the culture. All because of Callee. What was he thinking? He wasn't staying here. Or making a commitment to Callee. He would leave in a few weeks and not look back. So why did the idea make his chest tightened?

He had a job to do. Starting Monday, he had to finish up the interviews he had been doing and start wrapping up his research. At this point, he had to keep his eyes on the prize instead of worrying about his emotional attachment to Callee. There would be another woman in another town. What he feared was there wouldn't be another like Callee.

He kept an ear open during the day for Callee if she needed help. She'd been busy but not excessively so. A couple of times he stuck his head out to see if she needed him, but each time she'd waved him away.

At lunchtime he wandered up to the front of the clinic. She and Carl stood facing the TV.

"What race is it?"

"Fourth," they said in unison without looking at him. He moved to stand behind Callee. Tempted to touch, he resisted because Carl was nearby. She wouldn't like to appear unprofessional.

The horses left the starting gate. They ran in a group and slowly spread out, a few getting ahead of the others. Halfway around the track one horse took the lead. Another moved around three horses and came in behind the leader. The roar of the crowd, not very far away, seeped into the clinic. Dirt flew as the horses ran. They circled the turn closest to the clinic.

Callee backed into him. He didn't move. She trembled. Sadly, he didn't think it was because of him. Her attention remained totally on the race.

The horses continue down the backstretch then around the last turn and headed for the finish line.

Callee, along with Carl, started to shout for the lead horse.

Langston found himself caught up in the race, eager to see who would win as the horses raced side by side. He could see the splendor in the event as well.

When the second horse pulled ahead of the others and won the race, Callee turned around and threw her arms around his neck and jumped up and down. Right then, he believed he could become a fan of horse racing. "I have to admit it's easy to get caught up in a race."

Callee grinned. "I told you so." She stepped away from him. "With any luck we'll go out to the track to see the Oaks race."

"Which one is that?" Langston teased. He had listened and remembered what Callee said about the races. It was important to him that he be interested in what she was interested in.

Carl shook his head and walked back to his desk.

"You know which one it is. It's the one with the largest purse and the best horses." Her tone implied exaggerated patience.

Five hours later Callee popped her head into the office. "Hey."

He jumped.

"Sorry, I didn't mean to startle you. I don't have any patients right now. You want to watch the Oaks?"

"Okay, sure." He didn't care anything about the race, but he would go along.

"Then come on. It's about to start." She didn't wait on him.

He hopped up from the chair and hurried after her. She pulled the door open and kept going until she reached a spot near her usual one at the track fence. Others stood along beside them. People filled the center of the track. In the distance, he could make out the filled stands under the twin spires of Churchill Downs.

The air pulsated with excitement. Attuned to Callee he could feel her tremble beside him.

The track announcer said over the loudspeaker, "The horses are in the gate, and they're off!"

Those around them went quiet. Callee took his hand. Seconds later the horses thundered by them and out of sight. He had to admit it was enthralling for those few moments to see the jockeys in their bright colors and the power of the horses. "That's much better than watching it on TV."

"Just think what it's like from the grandstands. To see the entire field." The wistfulness got to him.

"Isn't it about time to close up for the day?" he asked.

"It is." She turned back to the clinic.

Carl joined them, stopping Langston from asking Callee about their plans for the evening. If they had any. He didn't want to assume there would be a continuation of their morning. He wanted Callee to ask him.

Back at the clinic Langston returned to the office to close out his work.

Callee entered a few minutes later. She pulled her purse from the drawer then hesitated, giving him an unsure look. "Uh… I'm headed home."

Langston reached for her hand and tugged her into his lap, giving her a tender kiss. "I've been thinking about doing that all day."

Her arm snaked around his neck. "You have?"

Langston kissed her again. "I have. I wondered if you'd like me to pick up some takeout. Maybe I could come to your place for dinner."

She smiled. "I'd like that."

He nudged her out of his lap and stood. "Good. How does lasagna, bread and salad sound?"

"Delicious."

"Then I'll pick it up at the Italian restaurant near me on my way to your place."

He kissed her again. She softened against him. How would he ever give this up? But he would somehow. He must in order to achieve what he wanted. Callee wasn't part of his life plan.

"You know for such a small woman you sure have a big weapon with your kisses. I'll do almost anything to have one."

She searched his face. "Is that a good thing or bad thing?"

Heaven help him, he feared it was the latter. "I'm not sure yet."

CHAPTER EIGHT

CALLEE FEARED WHAT was happening to her. She'd thought her and Langston's night together would be it. She should have known better. Here she was inviting him into her house once again and looking forward to the possibility of another night together.

She had spent the day working in a daze of memories, anticipation and fatigue. She was exhausted, but she couldn't fault the reason. A night with Langston was worth it. He had been tender, considerate as well as encouraging and demanding. Everything she wanted in a lover. Even more.

The way he had stood so close to her during the races, his body heat melding with hers, and the hot kisses left her with little doubt he still wanted her as much as she wanted him. The heady feeling of being desired by Langston made her nerves tingle.

She had taken a shower and pulled on a T-shirt and a pair of cutoff jean shorts by the time Langston rang the doorbell. She hurried to the door.

He stood there holding two large white bags.

"Let me have one of those. Did you buy enough for an army?"

He winked. "I thought we might need to keep our strength up."

Despite him having seen and touched all of her, heat still washed to her cheeks and turned them hot.

"I've got this." He headed toward the kitchen.

Langston had changed into something comfortable. He looked super sexy in his tight-knit shirt, well-worn jeans, and boots. How could the man wear something so simple and turn her on just by coming in the door?

"Callee, are you coming? I am starving."

"On my way." She entered the kitchen to see him unpacking the bags on the kitchen counter. Something about the picture made her pull up short. How easily they had slipped into being a couple. In two weeks she would be alone again. Wasn't she opening herself up to pain?

"I got us some cheesecake too. The lasagna is still hot. Let's eat before it gets cold."

"I'll get the plates," she murmured stepping around him.

Langston caught her by the waist. He studied her a moment. "Hey, you okay? If you don't want me here, just say so."

"I want you here, I do. It just seems like we're playing house pretty easily."

He let go of her. "I should go."

She placed her hand on his arm. "Please don't. I'm just tired. It has been a long day."

He gave her another long look. "Okay, I'll stay awhile."

"Good. I like company with my meals." She

went to the cabinet and removed two plates and handed them to him. While he served portions of lasagna onto their plates, she filled glasses with ice and tea, gathered tableware and napkins.

They ate their meal in polite quietness. She hadn't meant to create this uncomfortable silence. "It's all very good."

"Mama Marzetti is a good cook. She has taken care of me more than a few nights since I've been here." He dug into the lasagna.

Callee took a sip of her tea. "It figures you'd know her personally. Here I was wondering what you were doing in the evenings."

Langston forked another mouthful. "If you go in regularly, they get to know people."

"Somewhere in there I feel a little sorry for you."

He stopped eating and looked at her.

She shook her head. "You had to eat alone every night. I should have invited you to dinner. And you eat out so much that a restaurant owner has become a friend. I'm sorry."

"No need to feel guilty. I'm used to it."

She pursed her lips. "That's sad on a whole different level. I'm sorry that didn't sound very nice."

"No problem. It might be true."

"Anyway, I'm glad you met Mama Marzetti because I'm enjoying her food. I'll have to try the restaurant."

"Tell her you know me and I'm sure she'll give you a deal."

What he left off was, when he was gone. Why had she made it weird between them a few minutes ago? Because she was scared. Afraid he would carry her heart with him when he left.

Langston picked up a piece of bread. "Thanks for encouraging me to watch the races today. I found them interesting and exciting. I can't believe I've not seen one before."

"I just wish we could see the Derby race. But the clinic comes first. As soon as I left, someone would need medical attention."

"It usually happens that way." But her comment gave him an idea. A few minutes later Langston pushed back from the table. "I better go. I know you must be tired." He stood and picked up his plate. He took her empty one as well.

Do something. Say something. Callee swallowed. "Langston."

"Yeah?" He looked over his shoulder while placing the dishes in the sink.

"Don't go."

"Callee, it's okay. I'm good. I understand. I shouldn't have assumed anything."

"You didn't. I've just had a taste of what it would be like to have you all the time and I liked it."

Langston cleaned his hands and came to her. "I'm still leaving in a couple of weeks."

"I know. You never said different."

He cupped her cheek. "Can't we just enjoy each other while we can?"

She would rather have that than nothing at all. Somehow, she would figure how to survive after he left.

Langston groaned at the shrill sound of Callee's alarm clock going off. It was morning already.

Callee's head rested on his chest. She turned so he could see her face. "It's morning."

"Yep. It seems like we just went to sleep." His fingertips traced over her waist.

She yawned. "It wasn't but a couple of hours ago since we did. Someone kept waking me up."

"You started it."

Callee ran a hand over his chest. "Maybe I did, but you didn't fight very hard. Or at all, in fact."

He grinned. "I'm glad I didn't."

Callee kissed his chin. "I better get going. I have another long day ahead."

"I wish we could stay here for the day." He grabbed her hand and played with her fingers.

She looked back at him. "How about we make plans for that tomorrow?"

Langston kissed the tips of her fingers. "I'll hold you to it."

"I hope you do." She pulled her hand away and crawled out of bed. "Come on, it's time to meet the morning."

He groaned and pulled the covers up.

She nudged him. "Have you ever heard the saying you can't stay up with the turkeys if you want to soar with eagles?"

"Where did you get that one?"

"It's an old saying my dad uses meaning that you can't stay up all night and get up and be at your best the next morning." She went to the dresser.

He threw the covers back and got out of bed. "Whose fault is that?"

"You're blaming me? You're the one who woke me in the middle of the night." Callee looked at him in feigned shock.

"It wasn't my fault. You pushed that delectable bottom against me," he teased.

She put her hands on her waist. "I was only trying to get warm."

He grinned, standing straighter with his chin high. "I warmed you up, didn't I?"

She huffed and started toward the bathroom. "I'll accept half the guilt. The other is yours."

Langston chuckled. Everyone should be as lucky to wake to such stimulating conversation with a beautiful woman.

Callee looked up from the charts she had been working on when Langston said, "I have a surprise planned for you. I hope you like it. If not, we don't have to do it."

"What're you talking about?"

For the last two days, excitement and expectations hung in the air. The horses shifted in the stables, trainers, grooms and barn workers seemed to walk faster and talk excitedly. Langston continued his work on his interviews. Yet he would stop without hesitation to help her if there was a need. In a few hours that would be over. Derby Day would have come and gone.

"I've made arrangements for us to attend the last couple of races today."

"What? How?"

"I asked Dr. Bishop for permission. He agreed to send another doctor over so we could enjoy part of the day."

Carl came to the door. "Callee, there's someone here to see you."

"That must be Dr. Lawson, your replacement." Langston followed her up the hall. "I hope you don't think I've been too high-handed. I just wanted you to have a nice surprise."

Callee wasn't sure how she felt yet.

Langston stepped around her in the waiting area. "Hello, you must be Dr. Lawson. Thank you for coming. This is Callee Dobson who runs the clinic."

The white-haired doctor shook her hand.

Langston spoke to Callee. "We're just swapping places with Dr. Lawson. He was working in the stands. I thought it was a shame for me to be this close to a famous horse racing track and not even see a horse race. And you certainly should get to see it. Even Cinderella got to go to the ball."

Callee wasn't sure how she felt about this. Her gaze landed on Carl. He smiled and nodded. "Go."

"I can't go wearing jeans and a T-shirt. All those people in their hats and dresses."

"I fixed that as well. Again, I hope you don't mind. I ordered you a dress and hat. It should be here in a few minutes."

As if planned to the minute, the door opened and a deliveryman entered carrying a hatbox and a large square box. "I'm looking for Callee Dobson."

Langston walked over to him and took the boxes.

Carl said, "Come on, Dr. Lawson. I'll show you around. Hopefully things will be quiet until closing time."

The deliveryman left, and Langston offered the boxes to Callee. "If you don't want to go, we won't. But if you do you, have no excuse not to go. I'll abide by your decision."

"I don't know what to say." She wanted to see the Derby race, but Langston had done too much.

"Don't say anything just get ready to go." He gave her a nudge toward the hall. "You know you want to."

"But the clinic—"

"Dr. Lawson will handle it."

She looked at the boxes. "Okay, but I don't know about this dress. Where did it come from?"

"I ordered it from a boutique this morning. The saleswoman said it was just what you needed. That it easily fits a number of sizes. There's a hat to match. I understand you must have a hat to be completely dressed." He gave her another nudge. "Now go to your office and get changed. I have a golf cart waiting to take us over to the other side. I need to change too."

"You have clothes?" The man had thought of everything.

"I picked them up when I went by my apartment this morning. They're in the truck. Now stop asking questions and get dressed. I'll meet you right here in—" he looked at his watch "—twenty minutes."

"I'm going to agree this time, but don't make this type of thing a habit."

Langston grinned. "You have my word."

She carried the boxes to the office, placing them on her desk. She opened the larger one and pulled out a floral dress with large flowers in pink, yellow and green. The flowing material of the wrap dress had a ruffle neckline that crossed between her breasts and tied at her waist. She smiled. It was pretty and very feminine. She loved it. Beneath the dress were a pair of sensible pumps.

Callee then opened the hatbox. Inside she found a wide-brimmed white hat with flowers of the same colors as her dress around the rim of the hat. They matched perfectly.

"I hope they fit." Callee quickly removed her clothes. Minutes later she adjusted the tie at her waist. She moved one way then the other, letting the material flow around her. The dress was perfect for a spring evening at the races. She had never worn a hat, certainly not like the one Langston had given her. She pushed her hair behind her ears then placed the hat on her head. It looked wonderful as well.

With a smile on her face, she walked down the hall to meet Langston.

Langston felt like a king, seeing the look on Callee's face. She looked lovely enough to be queen of the Kentucky Derby. He smiled back at her, wishing he could always bring a smile to her lips like the one she wore now.

"I'm ready."

"Yes, you are." If Carl and Dr. Lawson hadn't been there along with a patient, Langston would have said more. He resisted the urge to kiss her. "Then let's go." He held the door for her to exit.

They settled in the waiting golf cart. As soon as they were seated, the driver took off.

Callee touched Langston's knee. "Thanks for doing this for me. What a nice surprise."

"You said you wanted to go. I thought it was something I could give you to remember me by."

She leaned against his side for a second. "As if I would forget you."

He swallowed hard. Maybe this was a bad idea. It would be a memory for him as well. "I thought we'd enjoy seeing the race together since we've never seen the Derby race in person before."

"Thanks. This is amazing. It's one of the nicest gifts I've ever received. How did you work all of it out?"

"This morning I spoke to Dr. Bishop and he gave his permission for you to go and found Dr. Lawson to cover for you. He also said that Mr. Sorensen has two extra seats in his box that he's willing to give us. We'll be right on the finish line. How does that sound?"

"Amazing." She wrapped her arm around his waist and squeezed.

"I like you in the hat. You look like a true Southern belle."

Callee batted her eyelids. "Well, thank you, kind sir."

The golf cart deposited them in the parking lot outside the grandstands.

"I hope you know where we need to go." Langston looked lost.

"If we're going to the main boxes, they're this way." Callee led him inside the grand old building. "Part of this building has been around for over one hundred years. The Derby is older than that."

They walked through and around the crowd.

Callee stopped and looked at the digital race board. "There's still plenty of time before the next race. Do you mind if we go by the paddock on our way? I'd like to see the horses up close."

"Sure. Whatever you like." Langston would give her whatever she wished except for him to stay.

Callee smiled. "This way."

She didn't stop until she'd worked her way up to the paddock fence. Langston stayed right behind her. She was so small, he was afraid he might lose her.

Callee looked at him. "Aren't they beautiful?"

He looked into her glowing face. "Yes, they are."

She turned back to watch the jockeys mount with the help of a groom supporting their leg.

He needed to leave soon. The more he was around Callee the deeper his emotions went. If he wasn't careful, he'd hurt her and possibly himself. In fact, he possibly passed that point already. But for today he would enjoy the time he had with her.

Callee led him under the stands. "We need to get to the elevator and ride up to the Spires Terrace & Suites floor. That's where Mr. Sorensen's box is."

They rode the packed elevator up then walked a flight higher. Along the way, Callee grabbed a booklet from a kiosk.

"What's that?" Langston looked over her shoulder.

"A program. It tells you all about the horses. How many races they've won. Their number. The jockey. How to place a bet. It's almost too much to absorb." She kept walking.

"Are we planning to bet?"

She shook her head. "I'm not. I could be fired

for that. I work too close to the jockeys and the horses, but I like pretending I can."

"When we sit down, will you show me how to read it?" He took her elbow, directing her around a group of people ahead of them.

"I sure will. We need to hurry. The next race will be starting in a few minutes."

They picked up their pace along a hallway going past an area with a buffet spread out, with people filling their plates. They continued on out to a terrace where people were lining the rail overlooking the finish line.

Langston stepped up behind her. "I thought we were sitting in a box?"

"No time to be social. The race is about to start."

Langston grinned. She had her race face on. He'd had more fun with Callee than he'd had in a long time. He placed his arm around her waist as the horses took off. He felt the excitement of the horses thundering past them and moving out of sight around the turn. They became a small pack of dots on the back stretch and far turn. They ran full-out as they came in front of the stands. The crowd roared as the pack closed in on the finish line.

Callee jumped up and down shouting as the race ended.

She would never leave this. The people, the horses, the excitement was too much in her blood to travel from place to place with him even if he would ask her. The realization saddened him. They just didn't want the same things in life. Yet, the idea of being a part of this made him long… No, that time had passed years ago.

"We can go find our seats now. There's about a thirty-minute wait until the next race. The Derby race won't start until six fifty-seven. We'll have quite a wait on that."

Callee led him to the hallway where the box seats were located. She stopped at the door where a security officer had been stationed. "I'm Callee Dobson and this is Dr. Langston Watts. Mr. Sorensen is expecting us."

The guard entered the room and soon returned. "You may go in."

Mr. Sorensen was there to greet them. "Glad you could join us."

"Thanks for having us," Langston said, shaking the man's hand.

Their host introduced them to the others there then said, "You're welcome to any empty seats and the buffet outside. Let the waiter know if he can get you anything."

Langston directed Callee to seats in the back of the very swanky box. It had glass windows that looked out onto the track and the large racing board with the lineup of horses for the next race. The seats were cushioned and comfortable and the floor carpeted. Langston knew that other sports had something similar but had no idea that horse racing did as well. If he thought about it, he should have realized. As Callee had once said, horse racing was a big money business.

"This is nice, isn't it?" Callee whispered close to his ear. She settled into a chair.

He liked the brush of her lips against his skin. "It is. How about explaining the program to me before the next race. I'd like to pick one to pull for."

She grinned. "You're starting to get into this."

"You know the saying when in Rome…"

Callee opened the paper booklet and leaned in close to him. She ran her finger across a column, pointing out different aspects of a horse and the jockey information. "This horse is a long shot. See how high the odds are?"

"So who do we pull for?" He studied the program. "I'm going with Mo' Money."

"I'm going with Texas Tall," she said without hesitation.

"I'm honored." For some reason her choice touched him. As if he were the one Callee would be pulling for.

"Do you mind if we go back to the Terrace to watch the race? I like the open air and the crowd."

"Whatever you like. This is for you." He stood.

"I do like my surprise."

"I'm glad. I hoped you would."

Callee led the way out of the door. They worked their way to the Terrace and found a spot on the railing. "I like to watch them loading the horses in the gate."

Once again, he stood behind her out on the Terrace.

Among the crowd was a boisterous man who was large in both height and bulk. He was dressed in a bright red blazer. His cheeks were a ruddy color almost as deep as his coat. He raised his arm above everyone with his glass in his hand, sloshing the liquid on those too close. He declared, "I put it all on Texas Tall."

Those around him cheered.

"He might have had too much of a good time," Langston commented, shifting Callee away as much as the crowd would allow.

Soon the horses were circling the track. When Callee's horse took the lead on the back stretch, she started jumping.

The man in the red coat became more animated.

Langston couldn't help but grin at her enthusiasm. He glanced at the man jumping around as well. With Callee against him, Langston felt the exhilaration and anticipation in her movements.

She grabbed his arm as she continued to bounce while yelling. She screamed, "Go, Texas Tall. Go!"

With the thunder of hooves, the horses came toward them. Callee's grip tightened on his arm. She continued to yell as Texas Tall crossed the finish line.

"He won. He won."

To Langston's surprise, she put her arms around his neck and gave him a smack on the lips.

He returned her kiss. "I could stand for you to win regularly."

Callee stepped back and looked around as if remembering her professional position. She smiled. "It had everything to do with the name."

"I don't know about that, but it did make the race fun to watch." If asked if his life was fun before today, he wasn't sure he could have answered positively. Callee had a way of making him enjoy whatever they were doing together.

"But I'm not as excited as that man."

Langston followed her look to the man in the red jacket. He hopped around holding a ticket high in one hand and a glass in the other. "I won. I won."

Seconds later the glass dropped to the concrete floor with a crash. People scattered. The man clutched his chest, groaned and fell with a hard thump.

A woman shouted, "Help. We need help here. We need a doctor!"

Langston didn't hesitate. He had no doubt Callee was right behind him as he fought his way through the crowd. "I'm a doctor."

Callee's hand remained on his back as he went.

The man lay on his back surrounded by broken glass.

"Everyone, please step back. Someone call 911." Using his foot, Langston quickly swiped away the larger pieces of glass so he could go down on his knees.

The man's face had been bright red moments earlier but had washed white. Blood ran from the back of his head.

Langston put his cheek to his mouth. A shallow breath came out of the man. Placing two fingers on the man's neck Langston checked for a pulse. None.

Callee moved across from him.

"Watch for the glass."

She brushed the floor with her foot before she got down to her knees.

"He's had a heart attack," Langston announced. He quickly shrugged out of his suit coat.

Someone behind him helped him remove it.

"Callee, see about his head while I start chest compressions. Use my jacket to stabilize his head. He had a hard fall," Langston told her. "Someone get the portable defibrillator. There's one inside on the wall."

He placed a palm of one hand on top of the other. Using the heel of his bottom hand, he applied pressure to the man's chest. Keeping count, he pushed down with a steady rhythm.

While he worked, he was aware of Callee checking the man's pulse, his respirations.

Someone above them said, "He'd been drinking heavy all day."

Langston sensed more than saw Callee tense. Was she thinking about what had happened before?

He glanced at her but didn't have time to reassure her. Determined he wouldn't let her experience that loss again, he renewed his efforts. He would see this man recovered.

Callee called, "I need a cloth here. Something to stop the bleeding." A waiter handed her a few cloth napkins. Callee placed a napkin to the back of the man's head. She then tied two napkin corners together creating a bandage long enough to wrap securely around the man's head, and tied it in place.

She returned to checking vitals. "I've got no pulse."

The portable defibrillator appeared at Langston's right side. He opened the man's shirt not sparing the buttons. Callee had removed the lead package and was preparing them for placement. She handed the first one to him.

"Clear," he called, and applied the charge.

Langston leaned back on his heels to watch the man. His eyelids flickered open.

"Lay still, mister. The EMTs will be here in just a few minutes. You'll be fine."

Langston picked up the man's wrist and placed two fingers, checking his pulse.

Callee adjusted the bandage.

"Make way. Give us room," someone from behind them said.

Moments later two medical personnel broke

through the crowd surrounding them. The group shifted. An EMT crouched in front of the patient. Beside Langston, another man took the same position.

"I'm Dr. Randell. We've got this now. You've saved this man's life."

Langston stood and watched as an EMT place an oxygen cannula under the man's nose. He stepped beside Callee who now stood at the man's head.

He squeezed her hand. "You okay?"

She smiled. "I'm better than okay."

"We make a good team."

"Yes, we do."

Too much so for his contentment.

They watched the EMTs load their patient onto a gurney and wheel him away with his family beside him.

Callee tugged at her dress, adjusting it. A large circle of blood stained it near the hem. "I'm afraid my beautiful dress is ruined."

"Callee, you're bleeding." Horror filled him. "The glass."

"I'm fine. It's just a little cut. I'm more concerned about my hat."

A woman handed it to Callee with a sad smile. The crown had been crushed.

"Oh, my poor hat." Callee popped the crown out, but there was a hole in the straw. She looked at him. "I know in comparison to saving a man's life my hat doesn't matter. It just makes me sad you gave it to me and now it's messed up."

"I'll buy you a new one. But right now we're going to see about your knee. I want to make sure there's no glass in it." Langston picked up his jacket. It was completely ruined. Blood and footprints were all over it.

"So much for my jacket." He stepped to the nearest trash can and stuffed the coat in it. "Let's go find a first-aid station and get your knee seen to. Then find a bathroom so we can get cleaned up." He took her elbow.

"We can leave if you want," Callee suggested.

"You don't want to see the Derby race?" He led her inside the building.

"I don't want you to feel like we have stay." She turned to the right.

"Honey, I want what you want."

She raised her chin. "Then let's clean up the best we can, have dinner and watch a great race."

Langston nodded. "Consider it done. First the first-aid station."

A staff member headed their way. Langston asked him for the nearest first-aid station or first-aid box. The man pointed to a bar across the room. There Langston got a box.

"Let's find a restroom where I can clean and patch you up." He looked around.

"You do know that you're making more of a deal out of this than it is."

He gave her a pointed look. "And you could learn to let someone care for you."

Callee cringed. Was she really that bad about letting someone do something for her?

"Now, let's find the restroom. We have a race to watch." Langston helped her up.

They found a single restroom. Langston went down on one knee to wash and clean the wound. His actions were gentle and caring. Each movement was tender.

"I'm not hurting you, am I?" He glanced at her.

"No." Callee watched his head bow over her knee.

"This might hurt." Langston ran a damp paper towel over the area.

"Ouch." She moved her leg.

Langston looked at the towel then showed it to her. "There was a piece of glass in there." He returned to cleaning the wound. Looking through the first-aid box he brought out antiseptic spray. "This may sting."

"I can handle it."

He gave the can a squirt. The spray covered the injured area. Callee sucked in a breath, held it. Langston waved cool air across the wound, cooling the sting.

"It's been a long time since someone did that for me. My mom used to when I was a little girl." The pain eased. "It feels better now."

"Good. I'm sorry I hurt you." Langston quickly

applied a perfect bandage. He kissed her on the thigh just above the covering.

Callee's heart swelled. Would she be able to let him go?

An hour later Langston escorted Callee back to the terrace to wait for the Derby race to begin. He listened to Callee sing "My Old Kentucky Home" at the top of her voice along with thousands of others in the stands. Some of her excitement of earlier had died with the adrenaline rush of an emergency, but the song returned it. They had agreed on a horse to cheer for with good odds but not the favorite.

During the race Callee yelled for their horse, which came in second.

Langston was happy either way. Because she was having such a good time. "We were close."

She smiled. "Yes, we were."

People hung around even though it had been the last race. "Why aren't people leaving?"

"They're waiting to see the ceremony in the winner's circle." She pointed across the track toward the race boards to a U-shaped area.

A number of people including the winning jockey and horse gathered there.

"That's the owner getting the silver trophy," Callee said. "That's the blanket of roses going across the horse's neck. That's why the Derby race is called the Run for the Roses."

"For someone who has never been to the Derby you sure know a lot about it."

"But because of you I can now say I have attended." Her eyes glowed with happiness. "If you're ready to go, I am too."

"I'm ready. You lead."

He and Callee worked their way around and through the crowd to where the golf cart had left them. One waited.

"How did you manage this?" Her expression was one of astonishment.

He winked. "I have my ways."

"I'm impressed."

"That's what I like to hear." He helped her into the cart.

They returned to the backside through the tunnel and were deposited at the clinic. Carl had already closed up. Despite the business of the day, the barn area was quieting for the evening.

"I need to go in and get my purse and clothes." Callee unlocked the door.

"I'll wait while you get those. Make sure you're safe." He stayed in the front.

"You don't have to do that. Until you came I handled it alone all the time."

Was she trying to get rid of him? Or remind him that he would soon be leaving? "Haven't we already established you don't have to feel responsible for everything? I'll wait."

Callee wasn't gone long, but she had taken the

time to change her clothes. She carried the boxes out with her.

He took the boxes from her. "I don't want to take it for granted, so I'm going to ask if I may come over tonight?"

"I hoped you would." She started toward her car.

His second of insecurity fled. Complete confidence was his middle name, so how did Callee always manage to keep him guessing?

Twenty minutes later she pulled into her drive and Langston parked behind her. He followed her into the house.

"I'm going to soak this dress and hope I can get all the stains out." She took the boxes from him.

"Hey."

She looked at him.

Langston dropped the boxes into a chair and opened his arms. She walked into them. "I've been wanting to do this all day. You were amazing today."

Callee tightened her arms around his waist and pressed her cheek into his chest.

He held her close, then kissed her. Could life get any better than this?

CHAPTER NINE

THROUGH THE NEXT week Langston settled into a routine he wouldn't have believed he'd have agreed to much less enjoyed. Or would have allowed to happen. He and Callee made love and showered together each morning. They then had coffee in her kitchen as they made breakfast and headed off to work. In the evening Callee cooked or he stopped for takeout. After their meal they watched TV, read, or played cards but mostly they fell into bed together, which he always found satisfying.

He taught her some Spanish words by kissing the parts of her body as he named them. She would repeat them by returning those kisses on his. He looked forward to those lessons all day long. He found living with Callee far too satisfying for his comfort. It baffled him how well he'd taken to the domestic life.

This had never happened before during one of his trips. There had been women he'd seen during those times but none who had him feeling so settled. On all the other jobs when it had become time for him to leave he had been ready. This occasion he dreaded having to tell Callee goodbye.

Just before they were going to bed on Saturday evening his phone buzzed. Looking at it he sighed. "I better get this."

By the time he'd finished his conversation, he found Callee in bed sound asleep. It was just as well. That phone call hadn't been one she would like hearing about. He was needed back in Dallas for new tests Valtech was running on a plastic he'd helped develop. It was unlike him, but he had asked to stay the amount of time he had originally planned. He was told no, he had to leave on Tuesday to make his meeting.

Now he had to figure out how to tell Callee.

He showered and slipped under the covers next to her warm soft body. He pulled her to him. She sighed softly. This was almost as good as having sex.

He was in trouble.

The next day Callee woke and stretched in the afternoon sunlight streaming through her bedroom window. She touched the hard, heated body lying next to her. She and Langston had slept late, made love and shared breakfast in bed to sleep once again.

What she would do when he left, she couldn't fathom. She would be lost. Yet, she would have to keep going somehow. Hadn't she done so when Joe had his accident, then died? She had moved on with her life. Or had she? She would survive the hurt of loss again somehow. At least she had another week or so to enjoy with Langston.

Langston nuzzled her neck. "Good morning."

She loved the sound of his low sexy voice. "It's afternoon."

He gave her a wolfish grin. "It goes fast when you're having fun."

"What do you have planned for today?"

Langston fluffed the pillow and placed it behind his back and leaned against the headboard. "I thought we'd stay in bed all day. Why? Do you have something else in mind?"

Too aware of the fact he would be gone soon she wanted to make the most of their time together. "I do have something I need to do this afternoon for a few hours."

Using his palm, he rubbed her stomach. "Want to tell me what it is?"

"Let's just say it's a surprise."

"I like surprises." His hand dipped lower. He kissed her.

An hour later they were in Langston's truck traveling down a narrow tree-lined road toward Thompsons' farm.

"There sure is a lot of nice fencing in this area," Langston commented as they passed one horse farm after another.

"That's because it's all about the horses here.

Barbed wire isn't used because that can damage the horse's coat. So as far as you can see there's nothing but wooden fencing."

"Impressive."

She directed Langston off the main highway for a couple of miles then told him to turn onto another country road. He drove down a pebbled drive lined by a white wooden fence that led to a house. They forded a running creek with trees hanging over it and kept going.

The two-story red brick Federal-style house she loved so much sat among large oak trees surrounded by pasture. The trim had been painted white. Ferns hung from hangers on the porch. The grass had been mowed to look like a golf green.

"What a nice place," Langston commented.

"Most people around here take great pride in the appearance of their farms. Mr. and Mrs. Thompson certainly do, but they're getting too old to handle it all. In fact, they've been talking about selling. If I had the money, this would be mine in a heartbeat."

"It's a beautiful part of the world."

She sighed. "Go past the house to the barn out back. You can park there."

He followed her instructions, stopping in a lingering cloud of dust outside the large red barn's doors. He lowered his chin and narrowed his eyes. "This isn't what I think it is, is it?"

She gave him a cheeky grin "And what do you think it is?"

"I think you're planning to get me up on a horse."

She tapped the end of her nose with her index finger. "You're so smart."

He looked unsure. "I don't know about that. And the Thompsons are what to you?"

"Landlords. Now friends. I needed a place to board my horse and I found them. They live closer than my parents." She climbed out and came around to meet him on his side of the truck.

He joined her. "So this is where you spend your weekends. I wondered. I had no idea."

"There's a lot of things about me you don't know." She wished he was staying around to learn them.

Langston stepped close so she was sandwiched between him and the truck door. He leaned close. His voice turned low and suggestive. "I know the important things. Like how sweet you taste." He gave her a quick kiss.

Disappointment filled her because there wasn't more.

"And how your skin quivers when I run my tongue over your hip bone." His hands went to her waist, the pads of his thumbs resting in the spot he just mentioned.

Heat shot through her.

His lips nuzzled her ear. "And best of all I know

how you sound when you scream my name as you come."

Her center pulsed with want.

Someone cleared their throat.

Callee jerked away from Langston with embarrassment making her stumble. Langston steadied her. She pulled at her shirt adjusting it where Langston's hands had worked above her pant line. "Oh, Mr. Thompson. I didn't hear you come up."

"Understandable." His eyes twinkled. "You were busy."

Her cheeks burned. "Uh… I'd like you to meet my friend, Dr. Langston Watts."

Langston reached out a hand. "Just Langston. It's nice to meet you, Mr. Thompson. You have a beautiful place here."

"It has been a good home for fifty years." The older man looked around with pride. "I don't want to keep you. I just wanted to say hi and let you know that Mrs. Thompson expects you to stop in for tea and cookies before you head back to town."

"We'll be sure to do that. We're going for a little ride this afternoon." She touched Langston's arm. "He's never ridden a horse so do you mind if we take Maribel?"

"Not at all. I'm sure she'll appreciate the outing. I'll leave you to it." Mr. Thompson started back toward the house.

Callee took Langston's hand. "Come. I'll introduce you to Maribel and PG."

"PG?"

"Pride and Glory. He's a descendent of Man o' War. One of the great horses in racing so PG was given a fancy name. I shortened it when Daddy gave him to me. PG missed the great running gene, but he's been a great friend. Especially after what happened to Joe."

Langston gave her a quick hug.

She tugged him toward the barn doors. "Come on. It's time for you to learn some horsemanship."

"Let's think about this for a minute." He didn't move.

"Langston, for a man who deals with the type of stuff you do all the time I can't believe you're scared of a horse. I promise you Maribel will be gentle with you. She would never hurt a fly."

Callee went to a stall and brought a horse out.

He looked appalled. "You're going to put me on Maribel? My feet will drag the ground."

"Would you rather ride Rebel? That big black stud over there." She pointed to the horse in the stall ahead of them.

"Maribel sounds like a lovely lady." He came toward her. "I'm sure I'll be able to ride her."

"I'm sure you've ridden a lot of things," Callee said with a cheeky grin.

His voice went deep. "I've let you ride me a couple of times today already."

Heat washed over Callee. She swatted his arm. "No more of that talk around the horses."

Over the next thirty minutes, Callee showed Langston how to approach and walk around Mirabel by putting his hand on her rump, so she always knew where he was, which really wasn't a problem since Langston stood a head taller than the horse. She then instructed him in the proper way of putting a bridle on, adding a saddle blanket and cinching the saddle.

"Now I want you to stand there and get to know Maribel. She likes to be scratched behind the ears and talked to. I'm going to get PG out of the stall and saddle him."

"Are you sure about leaving us alone together?" Langston sounded doubtful.

Callee shook her head, grinning. "You'll be fine. I'll just be right over here. Maribel doesn't kiss on the first ride."

Langston gave the horse's lips a dubious look. "Good to know."

Callee saddled PG. When they were ready to go, she dropped the reins of PG confident the horse would stay where he was. She returned to Langston. "I'm going to show you how to mount. Hold the reins, put your left foot in the stirrup and swing your leg over."

"I know those basics. I've watched western movies."

Callee dipped her chin. "Excuse me."

Langston followed her instructions, easily mounting the horse.

"Good. Well done, Maribel." Callee patted her neck.

"What about me?" Langston asked?

She patted his thigh. "You did good too."

"Thanks. Maribel and I both work well with praise."

"I'll keep that in mind." She returned to PG. "Do I need to tell you how to go and stop or have you got that covered from watching a movie too?"

Langston smirked. "Why don't you give me a refresher just in case I missed something."

"Take the reins in one hand. Nudge Maribel to go by touching her with your heels. Not too hard, she's a sensitive old soul."

"I'll keep that in mind."

Callee continued. "To stop pull back on the reins. Mostly she should follow PG with no problem at all."

"You sound very confident of that." Langston wasn't.

"Either way I'm right here beside you." She mounted PG.

Langston liked the sound of that. Callee meant while riding horses, but she was the type of person who stood beside the ones she loved. The kind who would wait no matter how long she had to wait. Her promises would mean something. But at the time Emily had meant hers. Yet, while he'd been gone she'd changed. And then, he'd changed.

Because he'd been so caught up in her betrayal with his best friend of all people. Why couldn't he see that before now?

He would never put Callee under those same restrictions. It hadn't been fair to Emily to leave and ask her to wait for him, and it certainly wouldn't be fair to Callee. Even now he couldn't bring himself to tell her he was leaving sooner than expected. He would find the right moment. Sometime. Today he wanted to give them at least a little while longer to enjoy their time together.

He secured the reins in his hand and gave the horse a bump with his heels, following Callee out of the dim light of the barn into the bright sunshine.

"We have a pretty day for a ride." Callee placed a hand on PG's rump and turned to look at him.

"Where're we going?" He wasn't sure he wanted to go far.

"We're going around the field. I usually check the fences for Mr. Thompson when I'm out for a ride. Then we'll follow the creek and come back to the barn."

The horses walked slow and close enough together that he could touch Callee. She rode with complete confidence, straight with shoulders back.

He tried to relax but couldn't completely let go of the saddle horn. Despite the amount of travel he had done and the different places he had been, this was a new experience on a different level. He had moved out of his comfort zone. He was learning he didn't always have to move around to experience life. Callee had led him into a whole other realm. He would've never thought doing a research project would have turned into such an enjoyable time. It was all because of her.

They rode through a copse of trees and came out on the other side to a small pasture area. They crossed it and arrived at the edge of a babbling brook.

"Is this the one I drove through?" Langston asked.

"It is. We're going to stop here and let the horses drink and have a rest. This is how you dismount." Callee grabbed the horn of the saddle, slung a leg over and came down on one foot. She brought the reins over PG's head. "Now you do the same. Remember it's important to hold on to the reins because if you don't and have a lively horse, it could get away from you. That's the last thing you need."

Langston climbed off the horse with a wobble at the end.

"That needs a little more practice, but you have the basics."

"Thank you, ma'am." Langston lifted the reins over Maribel's head. He had finally gained some confidence.

"Now we're going to lead them over to the water and let them drink. We don't want to overwater them especially if they're really hot."

Afterward they tied the horses to a tree. Callee took his hand and led him to a large rock by the water.

He sat and brought her down between his legs. Her back to his chest. Wrapping his arms around her waist, he rested his chin on top of her head. "It's gorgeous here."

"Like no other place on earth." A dreamy tone hung in her voice.

"That's how my parents feel about where they live in Texas too."

"That's not a bad thing. Oh, yeah, it's a restrictive thing as far as you're concerned. You know it doesn't have to be all or none. You can have roots and still see the world. People do it all the time. Life can be good with both."

"I realize that, but it hasn't really worked out that way for me."

"Have you tried it? Or even want to?"

This conversation had taken a turn he hadn't wanted to make. Was she leading him into promising something he couldn't or didn't want? On a pretty Sunday, by a babbling creek, in the warm sunshine, with the trees hanging over them and

Callee in his arms, he might say something he would regret. He gave her a light push. "Shouldn't we be going?"

She stood. Clouds of hurt filled her eyes before she blinked them away.

He and Callee were going to have to talk about his departure. Soon.

Leaving this time would be more difficult, but he would do so on Tuesday. They could remain friends. He might even visit if he was in town again. He'd let his feelings make decisions before. Feelings couldn't be trusted. His heart had controlled his brain then. Langston would no longer allow that to happen, as he was determined feelings would not dictate his life decisions.

They continued to walk the horses along the creek bank. He and Callee kept their thoughts to themselves, talking very little. When they arrived at the drive, they crossed it and stayed along the fence line until the barn came into view. They started toward the building, dismounting outside it.

"You're starting to look like a natural," Callee said, smiling.

He lifted the reins over Maribel's head. "That's what happens when you have a good teacher."

Callee proceeded to show him how to remove the saddle and bridle then where to store them. "After a ride a horse always needs to be groomed." She showed him how to do that as well. With that done, they put the horses back in their stalls. Callee washed her hands in the rain barrel beside the barn. "It's getting late. We need to go see Mrs. Thompson."

She waited while he cleaned his hands. They walked to the back door of the house. Callee knocked.

Mrs. Thompson opened the door. She smiled at them. "Hello, Callee. It's good to see you." She looked at Langston. "I heard you had a young man with you."

Callee made introductions.

Mrs. Thompson backed out of the doorway. "Come in, come in. I've got cookies made. We'll have a cup of tea."

Callee climbed the steps. "We can't stay long."

"You have time for a cookie and tea, I'm sure. Have a seat at the table. Nothing fancy here."

Callee took a chair, and Langston sat at the one next to her.

He looked around the relaxing room. If he was the settling down type, it was just the kind of place he'd like. A brick fireplace, a large wooden table and a country sink spoke of home. Even the big heavy stove looked wonderful. There was wooden wainscoting on the walls with warm yellow paint above. Everything about the place said people who lived here were happy. Before coming to Louisville and meeting Callee, would he have even noticed that?

"You and Mr. Thompson have a beautiful place."

"We have enjoyed living here. Raised our family here." She placed a plate of cookies on the table.

"The house is over a hundred and twenty years old. It's seen a lot in its time." The older woman turned back to the counter.

"Richard," she said, raising her voice, "Callee is here. Tea is ready."

Mrs. Thompson brought them cups and saucers.

"Can I help you?" Callee moved to stand.

Mrs. Thompson placed a hand on the younger woman's shoulder. "You just be a guest for once. So Langston, I can hear a Texas drawl in your voice. I'm guessing that's where you're from."

"I'm from a small town just outside of Dallas."

"What brings you to Kentucky?" Mrs. Thompson set the milk and creamer on the table.

Langston told her about his research.

Bringing a steaming teapot to the table, she poured them a cup. "That sounds like important work. I'm sure Callee has been very helpful."

"It's more like he has helped me. Langston is an excellent doctor." She looked at him. "I'm not sure what I'm going to do without him."

His chest tightened. Callee was making it harder for him to leave without looking back.

Mr. Thompson entered and joined them at the table. "I'm sorry. I was right in the middle of a newspaper article."

Over the next half an hour they enjoyed polite conversation.

"We should go." Callee stood and Langston did as well. "All the fences look good, Mr. Thompson."

"Thanks for checking them. They'll need to be in good shape when we sell."

"I'm going to call a Realtor in the next of couple weeks. I hate to do this to you, Callee, but you're gonna need to start looking for a place for PG. The family next door is going to take Mirabel."

She looked at her teacup as she turned it one way then the other. "I wish I could buy this place and keep Maribel, but it's just not possible. I've looked at the numbers and I can't swing it."

"I wish we could stay, but it has become too difficult to climb upstairs to the bedrooms. We need something all on one floor," Mr. Thompson said.

"I'm looking forward to moving closer to our children," Mrs. Thompson said.

Langston glanced at Callee. Her eyes held the same look of sadness that they had at the creek. He'd do anything to make that look disappear.

"I knew it was coming. I just didn't expect it to be so soon," Callee told them. "And I'll miss you both."

Mrs. Thompson took Callee's hand. "We'll miss you too, sweetie."

He and Callee walked to the door.

Mr. Thompson said, "I'll be in touch if something happens about the place. I'll give you as much time as I can to make arrangements for PG."

"I appreciate that. If all else fails, I can take him

home to Mom and Dad. I'd sure hate to do that. They're so far away."

She gave the older couple a hug. Langston shook their hands.

As Callee went out the door she said, "Mrs. Thompson, tea was lovely, thank you for having us."

"You're welcome, hon." She looked at Langston for a long moment then nodded. "Remember, young man, a good thing doesn't come our way often. Don't let it get away."

CHAPTER TEN

THROUGH THE REST of the evening and throughout the hours before dawn, Langston had thought often about Mrs. Thompson's parting remark. What had she meant? That remained an insignificant question compared to how to tell Callee he had to leave sooner than she thought.

Of course, he could stay. Maybe work it out so Louisville would be his home base. Yet, the idea of that scared him to death. What if it didn't work out with Callee just as it hadn't with Emily?

He would still have to travel. Would Callee wait on him to return? He couldn't take the chance he'd return to her and there would be another man in her bed. That devastation he couldn't survive again. But it had been his decision to leave before. It was his decision to do so this time. Shouldn't he bear some of the blame? If he'd been there for Emily, she might not have turned to Mark. Couldn't the same be said for leaving Callee?

But if what had happened with himself and Emily hadn't happened, then there would never have been a Callee. He couldn't imagine not having her in his life.

And what if they decided they didn't work? He

couldn't bring himself to even think about that hurt or hurting Callee. It would be best if they just parted and that was it. A clean sharp pain was always better than a long lingering ache.

Langston pulled Callee into his body. He would miss this until his dying day. If he stayed, he could have this every day. No, he couldn't think like that.

The alarm went off. Time for them to get up. He couldn't put it off any longer. The time had come to tell her. He jiggled Callee, using the arm around her waist. "We need to get moving."

"I know but I don't want to." She rolled to face him, burying her face in his neck and holding him tight.

Their lovemaking had been sweet and poignant the night before. As if Callee were marking him as hers. He feared she'd accomplished that mission.

"It would be nice to stay here, but we can't. Work calls."

Maybe he could just stay through the week. He couldn't if he must bein Dallas on Wednesday for the tests on the plastic. As it was he would cutting close with such a long drive ahead of him. If he stayed any longer it would just prolong the agony. They would call each other for a while, then they would get busy with their lives, and it would fizzle out to nothing. It's better and easier in the long run to cut it off and have a sharp pain instead of a lingering one.

"Callee, I've been trying to figure out how to

tell you this since Saturday night. I guess there's no good time and it can't wait any longer."

"What?" she murmured against his chin as she kissed it.

He backed away so he could see her face. "I have to leave tomorrow. That's what the call was about the other night."

Callee didn't say anything for a long time. She just squeezed him. With a burst of energy, she flipped the covers back and climbed out of bed.

Langston soaked in the view. A beautiful one he would think about every morning.

"Why didn't you say something sooner?" She grabbed her clothes.

"I didn't want to ruin a beautiful day yesterday or our time together last night." He gave her a pleading look. This was exactly what he hadn't wanted to happen.

"Or you didn't have the guts to tell me."

He grimaced as he put his feet over the side of the bed. "A little of both."

She glared at him. "You know it doesn't have to be this way."

"What're you talking about?"

"I'm talking about you leaving." She moved to the bathroom door.

"I don't know what you mean. You know I have work to do. That's what I've been called back to Dallas to do."

"No, I think you're running. You do know it's

okay to stay in one place. There are plenty of places close by where you could get data. Or you could travel out and return. You don't always have to be running."

"What brought this on?"

She took a moment before she answered. "I like you. A lot. I haven't let anyone into my life in a long time. Certainly not into my bed. I think we might have something special, but I don't know that we can do it long distance."

He started picking up his clothes. "I'm not doing long distance. I've been there done that."

She took a step toward him. "Yeah, but that wasn't with me."

"No, but I won't take that chance. You'd get tired of waiting around on me."

Callee came closer, a pleading look on her face. "You don't have much faith in me. Just because one girl didn't remain true doesn't mean I won't. You're just scared to try."

"That's not true." Or was it?

"Sure it is. You're just afraid if you care too much you'll get hurt, be disappointed. I think you're past that."

"This is our last day together. Let's not have an argument. Why can't we just part as friends?"

Her lips formed a line. "We can't have this discussion tomorrow because you'll be gone. The problem is you won't stay around to argue. You'd rather ignore the issue. Maybe that is the issue. You left before and because you did, your girlfriend found someone else. Could the problem really be that you don't want to take any responsibility for what happened? Has it ever occurred to you that just maybe you and your girlfriend wanted different things out of life?"

"Leave Emily out of this. You don't know what you are talking about!"

"Really? If you had been there, would things have been different? Maybe. Maybe not. But at least you would have known. It's easy to blame others when it should be ourselves we're looking at."

He took a step forward, glaring at her. "You're one to be talking. You've lived your childhood around your father and what he wanted then you changed your mind because of a sad accident you had nothing to do with. One you feel guilty over and refuse to deal with. Now you live your life for a man who is dead. You've found a place, the clinic, where you can do good to make up for something that wasn't even your fault to begin with, and you stay because it's comfortable and you're sure you can always handle the problem."

"You don't know what you're talking about." She turned and went into the bathroom.

He followed her to the door. "Then I'll give you an example. You're offered a job that's perfect for you, but you won't even consider it. Why? Because you're afraid you'll make a mistake in judgment. You're scared to step out of your comfort zone. Broaden your horizons, seize new opportunities."

"You seem to be well-informed about my life. I think you should spend some time on yours. Like eventually you'll have to give up your Peter Pan lifestyle. You'll have to go home and face your past so you can move into your future. When is the last time you saw your family? Or faced Emily? Or even Mark? What's the plan? Dodge them forever? Those are people you were supposed to love and care about."

"I have a job that keeps me moving. An important one. I have work to do."

She dumped her clothes on the counter and turned on the shower. "All excuses."

Disgusted he said, "This conversation isn't going anywhere. I'm going to my apartment. I have packing to do."

"With that you have a lot of experience," Callee spat.

He snarled at her. He picked up his duffel bag and stuffed the items he had kept at Callee's into it. "I'm sorry we couldn't have parted on a friendlier note."

"Yeah, it was fun while it lasted."

"Yep, right down to when it wasn't." He stalked out of the room down the hall and slammed the front door on his way out. With a roar of the truck engine and a satisfactory squeal of tires, he drove off. The very idea of Callee telling him he had a problem when hers dwarfed his by a long shot!

At his apartment he finished packing by cramming everything into his large bag. He looked at the bag and small duffel sitting beside the front door. Almost his entire life fit into them. For once he found that sad.

Langston made a few calls arranging to check out of the apartment. He let the hospital know he was leaving. The only thing left to do was to go to the clinic and wrap up his research papers. There were also three interviews he needed to complete. Two he would do today and the other tomorrow morning first thing, then he was out of town.

He drove to the clinic and pulled up beside Callee's car just as he had every day. A surge of grief overwhelmed him. He put his arms on the steering wheel and his forehead on his hands.

He didn't want to leave things between him and Callee in such an ugly mess. He cared about her, more than he had ever cared for a woman. Even Emily. But he couldn't let that affect his decisions. He had done that before and what had it gotten him. Nothing but a broken heart. He couldn't take the chance on it happening again. He wasn't ready to give what Callee demanded and needed.

Climbing out of his truck, he squared his shoulders and walked to the clinic. Maybe Callee had settled down some. He entered the building. She was talking to Carl. She didn't look at him before she ended the conversation and walked down the hall.

Was she not even going to talk to him again? How quickly things had gone from blissfully happy to complete devastation.

He wished Carl, who had a perplexed look on his face, good morning and went to the office. He passed an exam room where Callee fiddled with some supplies. He knew full well she was dodging him.

Langston spent the morning organizing his research then went out after lunch to find the two jockeys he needed to interview. He returned to learn from Carl that Callee had left to check on Gina, who had returned to work. Langston explained to Carl he was leaving in the morning, that he would be coming by to do one more interview and he would then leave for Dallas.

That evening he drove to his apartment, the empty, sterile one with no light and happiness in it, for the night. The entire day had been tense, drawn out and miserable. Callee had treated him like he never existed.

The night was worse than the day. He couldn't sleep. Finally giving up on the bed, he moved to the sofa with no luck. He ended up watching TV until it was time to go to the clinic. With his two bags in the back of the pickup truck, he was ready to drive away as soon as he finished the interview.

Langston finished his interview and examination of the jockey in one of the exam rooms. Once he'd left, Langston went in search of Callee. He would not leave without telling her goodbye. He found her in the office. "Callee, can we talk?"

"I think we've already done that." She looked at the computer instead of him.

"I have more I want to say, ask really. If I asked, would you come with me? I'm sure my company could find a place for you."

"Please don't. Anyway, it really wouldn't make a difference. You don't want me following you around, and I don't want to be one of those women."

"What do you want? For us to call each other daily, which would go to every other day, to once a week, until we're too busy to speak to each other. Maybe I could stop in every once in a while, but even that would get old. It's better to cut it off clean. It won't hurt as much, I promise."

"That's right, you've done all this before."

The bite to her words hurt. He had, but with Callee it was much harder. The pull to stay stronger. But it would do her no good, or him either if he stayed. In the end he would still leave.

He sighed. "Then I'll say thanks for sharing your clinic with me. I'll be leaving now. Walk me to my truck?"

Her sad gaze met his. She shook her head. "I'd rather not. I hope you have a good life."

Disappointment flooded him.

She turned her attention back to the computer.

Langston headed up the hallway his shoulders heavy with remorse. He didn't like leaving this way. Maybe it was just as well. It would be better to just leave and not hang on to their relationship than to later watch it slowly die.

At his truck, he had opened the driver's door when a golf cart flew to the front of the clinic and jerked to a stop. A man, scraped and bleeding, sat in the back seat. He held his arm as if it were broken.

Langston loped back to the clinic. Callee would need his help.

Regardless of Callee's best intentions, she followed Langston up the hall. She stood at the door, watching him walk to his truck. She wouldn't cry. It would only make it harder to let him go. She would be strong. The last thing she wanted Langston to remember was her sobbing. Or begging him not to go. She was better than that.

Callee didn't want a man who didn't want her. She wanted one who would be there in the morning, every morning. She'd already lost one relationship. She didn't want to lose another.

A golf cart stopped in front of the clinic doors, drawing her attention. She hurried to the bloody man in the back seat. Helping him to stand she said, "Come on, let's get you inside and taken care of."

The driver went to his other side and between the two of them they managed to get the man inside.

Carl had left early for an appointment so she would have to handle this herself.

"Callee?"

Langston was back. How many times was she supposed to live through him leaving? Why hadn't he kept walking?

Seconds later he entered the small room, making it feel smaller. "What happen here?"

"Bike accident."

He shook his head. "It must have been some accident. What can I do to help?"

"I thought you needed to leave." She didn't like her own bitter tone.

Langston gave her a hard look. "You need my help."

Callee's disappointment ebbed away. He would always come if she needed him. Langston moved to one side of the man and she to the other. "We need to get him on the exam table."

They helped the injured man up. There were very few visible areas that didn't have a scratch or a gash. Mangled was the only way to describe him. The misery in his eyes matched his damages.

"I'm Callee and this is Langston. And you are?"

"Rodriguez."

"Sorry we have to meet this way." Langston was

in the process of cutting the man's shirt off him. "What happened, Rodriguez?"

"I was riding a bike. A truck pulling a trailer hit me. Knocked me into a barn then to the gravel."

Langston shook his head. "All this from a bike accident."

Callee gathered supplies and brought them into the room. "Bikes arc a good mode of transportation around here, but this happens so often."

"That's a shame."

"Rodriguez, we'll—" she looked beyond the man to Langston, meeting his gaze "—have you cleaned up and bandaged in no time." She tried for a positive smile.

Langston nodded and went back to putting scissors to their patient's shirt while she set up the saline, bandages and instruments on a tray.

"I never saw anybody with quite so many superficial cuts and scrapes," Langston said in wonder. "They are shallow but everywhere."

The man winced and jerked his arm. "Sorry."

Together she and Langston finished removing the shirt. The man stiffened.

"Sorry about that, Rodriguez. We'll soon get you straightened out. Just as quick as we can."

"I have to get back to work." Rodriguez looked toward the door.

"I'm afraid this isn't going to happen for a while, but right now we need to exam you and see if you need any stitches." Callee worked to reassure the patient.

"I'll take care of vitals. Mind if I borrow your stethoscope?" Langston asked.

She pulled it from around her neck. Their fingers brushed as she handed it to him. That same shot of awareness raced through her. Would that ever change? Heartache quickly followed.

"You got to cut my pants?" Rodriguez asked.

"If you are up to removing them yourself, then we won't have to."

Rodriguez nodded. "I can handle it."

"Then Langston will help you while I get you something to wear." She stepped out of the room, sensing the young man wanted privacy. "I'll be right back."

Callee returned to find Rodriguez sitting on the exam table with a hospital gown on. She went to work examining him. "There were many abrasions and scrapes, but it doesn't look like you'll need any stitches, which is good. In fact, the only ones we will bandage are the larger ones. The others will remain uncovered. But I will want you back here to check for infection every other day."

"May I check out your head?" Langston asked.

Rodriguez nodded.

Langston stepped in front of him and pulled out his penlight. Shining it into his eyes he said, "Please follow the light. Good. Now look at a spot over my left shoulder. Don't move. Good."

Pulling on examination gloves Langston said, "Now I'm going to run my hands over your head. Let me know if anything hurts." Slowly he worked his fingers over Rodriguez's skull.

The man flinched.

"It hurts right here?" Langston looked closer at Rodriguez's head.

"Yes."

"Okay. There's a knot. It's coming out so that's good. If you have any headaches, eye bleariness or trouble walking, come see Callee right away." He met Rodriguez's look. "Do not wait. Understand? You should go for a head scan at the hospital. You took a real tumble. Callee will help you with that."

"I understand."

Callee would miss this Langston too. The one who truly cared about his patients. His abilities were wasted on nothing but research. He was too good with people.

Over the next hour she and Langston cleaned and bandaged the wounds needing their attention.

When they'd finished, Rodriquez gave them a weak smile. "I look like a mummy."

She grinned. "You sure do. You need to keep the bandages clean and dry. Come see me before the weekend."

"I need to work."

Callee shook her head. "Not in a barn."

When Rodriquez started to say something, she stopped him. "I know, but you're gonna need to let somebody else handle the hay and grain. The airborne stuff can cause infections. You'll have to take a few days off and then be only outside. No mucking."

She caught Langston checking his watch. "I appreciate your help."

"I'm sorry I have to go." His eyes held shadows of concern.

"I understand."

Langston said, "Rodriguez, take care of yourself. Be careful on a bike."

Langston gave her another searching look before he touched her on the shoulder then went out the door.

CHAPTER ELEVEN

THE DRIVE FROM Louisville to Dallas was long and lonely, giving Langston plenty of time to think. Not what he really wanted to do. His chest felt tight since he pulled out of the parking lot of the backside hours ago. He didn't like the way he and Callee had parted. Yet he feared if he'd allowed them to continue seeing each other, he'd never be able to leave her. Even now he wasn't sure he could survive without her.

He replayed their conversations, over and over. Was he running? Not taking some of the blame for what happened with Emily. And Mark. He had accused Callee of hiding but wasn't he just as guilty? Staying on the road and not facing his past? He made it an art form to stay away from the town where parents and Emily and Mark lived. He'd taken all those jobs because he didn't want to face the past and his hurt.

The farther he drove away from Callee the tighter his chest became. He would learn to live with the ache. Surely it would go away in a few days.

Tired and emotionally drained, he stayed in a hotel for the night believing he would get a good night's sleep. Instead, he tossed and turned, and was miserable. Another night of sleep missed. He blamed it on being in a different bed, but he knew better. It was because Callee wasn't there. Too many times he had reached out to pull her to him and been disappointed to find nothing but a cold pillow beside him.

The late heat of Dallas made sweat pop out on his brow. He already missed the spring breeze and green trees of Kentucky. Wednesday evening after the meeting he just made in time, he entered his apartment and went stock-still. He dropped his bags with a thump.

The place looked as sterile as an operating room. There was no life in it. None of the warmth of pillows, soft lighting, or the colors of Callee's home. Nothing about it looked welcoming or lived in. Or even cared for. It was completely the opposite of Callee's place. And his heart felt just as cold and empty as this place.

Langston turned around and walked out, unsure of what to do. In his truck again, he started to drive. To his surprise he ended up in Prairie. At the welcome sign posted at the town limits, he pulled over and looked at it. It had been years since he'd returned. He'd made excuses not to. His parents visited him when they came to Dallas, or he met them somewhere for dinner but he hadn't been to town since Emily and Mark had told him they were getting married.

The town had been a good place to live. He'd grown up happy there. But he'd let bitterness control his life. Because of that he'd punished his family by not visiting them. He'd let that pain overshadow all the good of his childhood.

That happiness he'd had so long ago had returned while being with Callee. It was the first time since childhood he'd felt he belonged. Even had a sense of being a member of the backside family. If he wanted that feeling back he had work to do. He had to face his past. That meant he needed talk to Mark and Emily. His mother had once told him Mark and Emily had moved into Mark's parents' house after they'd moved to the coast.

He pulled in front of the house with the white picket fence. Emily had always talked about wanting one. He'd always thought they were a sign of being settled, as a restriction. Yet he hadn't seen the white fence around the Thompsons' farm like that. There he'd seen the fence as protection of something of value.

The idea of being fenced in with Callee didn't make him want to run now. Somehow the idea made him feel secure. As if he'd found the place he belonged, where someone would always be waiting on him to return and would be happy to see him. Had Callee been right about him and Emily wanting different things out of life back then? Were they just not meant to be?

Langston parked on the road in front of the

house. He walked to the front door and knocked. Would they be glad to see him or close the door in his face?

Mark answered the door. He looked older and settled. He'd always been the home body of the two of them. His temples were graying. giving him a distinguished look.

Mark's eyes widened. His face paled in disbelief. "Langston."

"Hi, Mark. I'm sorry I didn't call first, but I didn't have your number." Langston heard sounds of children playing in the backyard. "I was wondering if we could talk for a few minutes. I won't take a lot of your time."

Mark looked behind him, concern etching his features. "Come in. Emily's in the backyard with the kids. We're getting ready to grill hamburgers."

"I didn't mean to interrupt your mealtime. I can come back later."

"No, no. Now is fine. I know Emily will be glad to see you. I certainly am." Mark led him down a hallway to the back of the house.

"I won't stay long."

"How have you been? When I see your mother or father in town they proudly tell me where you have been and everything you have been doing. I'm not ever surprised. You were always an achiever and eager to leave this town."

Langston looked at the house as they walked through it. He remembered the 1960s layout, but

Emily had made a number of changes, along with the very lived-in space that included shoes, book bags and toys. The feelings were the same ones he got at Callee's minus the children's paraphernalia. As if the people who lived here loved each other.

They continued out the glass back doors to the patio. A boy and a girl played on a wooden swing set. Emily stood nearby watching them.

"Emily," Mark called.

She turned, and her mouth dropped open as a look of astonishment covered her face moments before a smile formed on her lips. "Langston!" She started toward him. "Louise and Willy, come here. I'd like you to meet a friend of ours."

Langston returned the smile, felt it ease the tension that had filled him.

"What a nice surprise. It's good to see you."

Emily looked just as she had before with a few more lines around her eyes but still a cheerful mild mannered person. Nothing like the strong, self-assured, sassy Callee.

The boy and girl came up and stood beside their father. "Kids, I would like for you to meet one of our friends. This is Dr. Langston Watts."

Langston went down on his heels, meeting them at eye level. "It's nice to meet you. Your mother and dad and I used to be great friends."

The girl the obvious elder of the two said, "We know who you are. Mom and Dad talk about you. You are the doctor."

Langston glanced at Emily and then Mark.

"They tell stories about all the fun things you did around town growing up. They laugh about them even when it isn't funny."

That touched Langston's heart. Why had he waited so long to do this? They did share wonderful memories of living in a small town where they wandered around not having to always be on guard. Where they knew everybody, and everyone knew them. He'd let the bitterness of what had happened between Emily and him overshadow everything. Including his relationship with his parents and how they'd chosen to live their lives.

"Yeah," the boy said. "They tell me to study hard if I want to be a great doctor like you. That you help people."

Langston's heart warmed. Emily and Mark had used him as an example to their kids. Wow, that was high praise. Too high after the way Langston had acted. "You do have to study, but it's all right to have fun sometimes too."

Emily spoke to the children. "Go play while the grown-ups talk. We'll eat in a few minutes." She then led him over to a picnic table with Mark, where Mark and Emily sat beside each other.

They looked like they belong together. Someone at the ball had said he and Callee looked like they belonged together.

"Thanks for letting me in."

"I have to admit I was a little more than surprised to see you." Mark took Emily's hand and gave it a squeeze.

"I didn't exactly plan this."

"So why after all this time are you here?" Mark asked.

Langston looked from Mark to Emily and back again. "Because I owe you both an apology."

It was the couple's turn to look at each other.

"I acted poorly. I've carried a grudge." He looked at Emily. "At first, I was mad you didn't wait on me. But the truth is I left you behind." His focus went to Mark. "For too long I believed you took Emily away from me. But I can see now y'all belong together. I finally see what you saw. We wanted different things. I just wanted to apologize for being such a jerk and staying away so long. I've missed your friendship."

"Your reaction was natural. We've been hoping that you would change your mind and at least speak to us. Thank goodness you have. You needed to go, and I needed to stay." Emily glanced at her children.

"What made you change your mind?" Mark asked.

Emily smiled and spoke before he did. "He's met someone."

"I did." But would she have him back? After he left her, just as he had Emily?

"I've been telling Mark for years that all it would take is for you to find the right one and you would understand, forgive us." She looked pleased with herself. "It's finally happened. So tell us all about her."

"Callee's the PA at Churchill Downs' backside clinic. She smiles all the time. Knows everyone. Can handle horses. Looks great in a ball gown." And was perfect for him. Why hadn't he realized that before now?

"I found the right man for me and apparently you've found the right girl for you." Emily leaned her shoulder against Mark. "I'm glad."

"Would you like to stay and have supper with us?" Mark asked.

Langston stood. "I better not. I still have to see my parents. May I take a rain check?"

Emily nodded. "Only if you promise to bring Callee by to meet us."

"You have my word." That's if he could get her to forgive him.

Fifteen minutes later he knocked on the kitchen door of his parents' home. Before his mother could get there to open it, he walked in.

"Langston!" his mother squealed, and dropped the knife she'd been using to peel an apple.

"Hi, Mom."

His father came in from the other room. "Dad."

His mother rushed to bring him into a hug. Tears filled her eyes. Guilt washed through him. He should have made it a point to see his parents more often.

Langston's mother let him go seconds before

his father hugged him, slapping him on the back. "This is a wonderful surprise."

"A real nice surprise." His mother continued to touch his arm as if she feared he wasn't real.

"Sit down and I'll get you a cup of coffee. Have you eaten yet?"

"No, Mom, but I'd like to take you guys out for a meal."

His mother shook her head. "No, no. I was working on an apple pie and your father requested pork chops. There's plenty for us all."

"She's still the best cook in town." His father looked at his mother with such love.

It was similar to those Callee gave him. Why hadn't he seen it before? Because he didn't want to believe it. Didn't want to examine his own feelings.

His mother brought the coffee, filling his cup.

"Mom and Dad, I owe you an apology." He was saying that a lot lately.

"For what, honey?" His mother looked concerned.

"For not coming home as often as I should."

"We understand that your work is important." His father picked up his mug.

"Not more important than the ones I love. I let my feelings about Emily and Mark affect my actions. You didn't deserve that. I'm sorry. I was so wrong."

"You were hurt. We understood that." His mother's fingers clutched the back of one of the kitchen chairs.

"Still, that was no excuse. I went to see Emily and Mark."

"How did that go?" his father asked.

"We are good."

"I'm glad to hear that." His mother's voice held such relief.

"Mom, Dad, I could use your help with something."

Langston told them about Callee and how he'd left things between them. Since having a taste of the warmth and the feeling of belonging that he had with Callee, he realized what he'd been missing in life. He wanted it back. He wanted Callee.

At times Callee hadn't been confident she would survive the week after Langston left. She had looked for him at every turn, then had hoped he would return, while crying herself to sleep each night. She had already lost too much sleep in her life over something she couldn't change. Joe. Now she was doing so again over Langston.

He had broken her heart. And she'd let him.

Not even after Joe's accident had she been this devastated. Only in the last few weeks since Langston had come to town had she'd been able to talk about Joe without being shackled by guilt. Because of Langston she'd started living again. Finally accepting she couldn't have done any more for Joe than what she had done. It felt good being released from those bonds.

But the crying had to stop. Langston wasn't coming back. Thank goodness she'd been too busy to watch him drive away. She would have been a blubbering mess. He wouldn't have liked that, and she wouldn't have either. Instead, she'd gone home and fallen apart.

It had been difficult for her to function at work without sleep. She disliked mopey people and she had become one of them. She kept one foot in front of the other. Barely.

Callee now understood why she'd kept other men at arm's length for so long. This pain was excruciating. She hadn't allowed her other relationships to move past the friend stage on purpose, stuck in her pain and her guilt, but Langston had pushed that barrier out of the way.

It was time for her to pick herself up. She had been through loss before. She could, she would survive this one.

Dr. Bishop had stopped by one day to ask her how it was going and how things had been with Langston helping out. Callee shared that everything had gone smoothly. For a brief second, he studied her a little closer than she would've liked. Had he noticed their closeness at the ball or the tightness around her mouth? Could he see the gaping hole where her heart had been?

More than once she'd noticed the concern in Carl's eyes too. It took him to midweek after Langston left before he asked, "Have you heard from Langston?"

"No."

"I sure liked having him around. Good doctor," he said causally as he watched her too closely.

"Yes, he is."

"Do you think he'll come back?"

She snapped, "No."

"I'm sorry, Callee. It's his loss."

She hated the sympathy in his voice. Hated that she cared. They were the last things she wanted. Her eyes watered. She turned and headed to her office.

After that Carl said no more about Langston.

Determined to snap out of the Langston-induced funk, she tried to keep her regular schedule, which was to go visit her parents the next weekend, but she couldn't bring herself to do anything more than go to work and then crawl into bed. She did manage to call. After all, she needed to make arrangements for PG to go home until she could find another place to board him closer to her.

Her mother's voice was a balm to Callee's soul. "It's so good to hear from you. It's been too long."

"I know, Mama. There was Derby Week. And you know how that is and then other things came up. Sorry. I'll be out to see you soon."

"I'm just glad to hear from you."

Emotion filled Callee's throat. She was too. "Is Dad around? Can I speak to him?"

"He's on a run. He should be home soon."

Callee looked around her bedroom. "He always seems to be on a run. He needs help."

"Yeah. But he can't seem to find someone he trusts."

"I let him down, didn't I? He'd planned on me helping him." Callee used to go with him. She loved every minute of the time they spent together.

Her mother sighed. "You didn't let him down. It was more like disappointing him. But you know how your father is when he makes up his mind about something. It's hard to change it." Her mother paused. "You want to tell me what's going on?"

Callee fiddled with the edge of the blanket on the bed, bringing it to her nose. It smelled of Langston. "Just the same old stuff. Nothing special."

"I can hear in your voice something is wrong."

Was Callee's unhappiness that obvious? "Why do you say that?"

"Because I am your mother and I know you."

Callee blinked to control the moisture threatening leak from her eyes.

"Telling me about it, honey."

That was all it took for Callee to let her emotions spill out to her mother about Langston. Before she finished Callee's words were gasps. "I haven't heard from Langston since he left. We had a big fight. He said a lot of things about me and my life that I didn't want to hear."

"Such as?"

"That I can't talk to Dad about my feelings and that I've let the situation with Joe control my life."

Her mother's voice softened. "Honey, I have to agree. I think you've carried responsibility for Joe's accident and death for far too long.

"Your father's home. Let me take the phone to him. You two need to talk. You should tell him how you feel."

That didn't sound like fun to Callee.

"After you do that, I suggest you think long and hard about what you want out of life. What you want it to look like. Only you can decide that. Here's your dad."

Callee's palms started to sweat. She sat up on the edge of the bed.

"Hey, Callee girl. How are you?" Her father's voice said he was pleased to hear from her.

Had he always greeted her like that? Why hadn't she noticed before? Did her concern over disappointing him color her view of her father? Maybe she was the one who needed to see things differently. "Hi, Dad."

"It's been a while since I've been home. Your job must be keeping you busy. We miss you around here."

"I'm sorry about that, Daddy. I'll be home soon. What kind of case did you have today?"

"An old mare with a cyst on her neck."

She heard the bang of the storage door on the side of the truck. Her father was putting equipment away. "I always loved going with you on your runs."

"Yep, then you turned to human medicine."

"But I learned so much from you that I use every day on people, like compassion, talking softly when they've shared, to how do I get them to do what I need them to do. All that I learned from you."

There was a pause as if he were thinking about that. Now was the time to say it. "I know I disappointed you when I changed to human medicine. I'm sorry for that but I'm where I belong."

"I was disappointed. I let myself have big plans for sharing my practice with you. But I was thinking about me and not you."

"I had thought at one time I would join you too."

"I resented you for changing after Joe. I guess I thought in a way he took you away from me. Then I saw you blossom when you talked about your work. The passion you had for it that was beyond even that which you showed for animals."

It had been that way. She had fallen in love with caring for people. It had fed a part of her that she hadn't even explored because she had been so caught up in thinking about being a veterinarian.

"I heard what happened with the horse in the trailer. Also, the horse with the flu."

"You did?"

"We vets talk. Especially when my daughter is involved."

She heard the pride in his voice. The cold she had been feeling started to warm up a bit. "Small world."

"I am proud of you. I'm proud of the quality work you do. Along with the person you are."

"Thanks, Daddy. I needed to hear that."

"I also heard you had a big deal doctor working with you for a few weeks."

Langston. She wasn't sure she could talk about him with her father. It had been all she could do to discuss Langston with her mother. "Yes. I didn't realize what a big deal he was." In more ways than one. "But he's gone now."

"Will he be coming back?"

She looked out the window to the sunny day beyond. "I doubt it."

"Sounds like you might have liked him."

"Yeah, but he's gone now." Gone. She didn't like the sound of that. "I've been offered a new job."

"You have?"

"It's working with the jockeys and the horses. Studying their interactions. It's a new program that Churchill Downs is supporting where I'd do the care for the jockeys, but I'd also be in on their work with the horses. It would be the best of both worlds for me. I wasn't going to take it but I'm rethinking that. Dr. Bishop is encouraging me to do it. A Dr. Mitchell would be one of the lead people on the program. In a few years I might have the opportunity to run the program."

"Sounds like it would utilize your skills."

"But I like where I'm working." She did. So much she couldn't see beyond it.

"It's easy to stay where you're comfortable. It's much harder to stretch yourself."

"Someone else said the same thing to me the other day." Langston.

"I think you can do anything you put your mind to. You need to think about what you want and what uses your skill set." Her father's voice had turned firm.

"Now you sound like my mother."

His tone held warmth when he said, "Your mom's a smart woman."

Her parents had been together since they were teenagers. They had a home and raised their family, but they still loved each other. What could she do to have that?

Callee's tears had cleared during her conversation with her parents. It was time for action, change. To move toward, to go after what she wanted.

Langston had been right. She'd been using the clinic to hide, had created a cocoon where she didn't let herself make mistakes. She didn't take chances out of fear. She would look into the job opportunity. See what it involved.

It was past time for her to pick herself up and move on.

* * *

Langston pulled through the stone gateposts into the drive of the Thompsons' farm. Since it was Sunday afternoon, Callee would be there to see PG. Would she be glad to see him? He hoped so. His happiness and life plans depended on it. It had been a long emotional week since he'd last spoken to her. He couldn't complain; he was the one who said it would be best to cut it off clean. His words had come back to bite him like a rabid dog.

He'd promised not to contact her, and he'd kept his word but it almost killed him. The number of times he picked up his phone with her in mind went into the hundreds.

Would she hear him out? Was she still angry with him? Would she be as excited to see him as he was her? Had he spent too much time reorganizing his life when he should have been begging her to take him back? The questions ricocheted around in his head.

His heart beat faster the closer he drove to the house. His palms sweated against the steering wheel as he drove past the house and pulled up next to Callee's car parked outside the barn. Relief washed over him. She was here. Mrs. Thompson had told him to hang on to a good thing. He hadn't listened at the time. Now he knew exactly what she had meant. If Callee would have him, he'd hold on tight this time.

After returning from Prairie, the first call he

made was to Valtech headquarters to propose opening a permanent location in the Louisville area. He volunteered to start the program along with creating an affiliation with the University of Louisville to further study sport safety. That took some persuasion, but he managed an agreement. He also contacted the hospital in Louisville for permanent privileges. The board eagerly agreed to let him be on staff.

His last and final call had been to the Thompsons asking if they would hold off on the selling of their home until he could talk to Callee. If she agreed, he hoped they could make it their home. The Thompsons had agreed to wait.

He hoped his plans didn't backfire. All that had to happen was for Callee to turn him away.

Climbing out of his truck, he took a deep breath and rolled his shoulders. He walked into the dim light of the barn more nervous than he'd ever been.

Callee was halfway down the hall. PG stood between them so she couldn't see Langston coming. While she brushed the horse, she talked to him. "It's time to move on, ole boy. For both of us. We both need a change."

She leaned down toward the horse's belly, paused and popped up. Stepping around PG's head, she stopped. Even in the dappled light Langston could tell her eyes had widened.

"Langston." His name was a little more than a whisper.

"Hi, Callee." He stepped closer.

"What're you doing here?" His reception was cooler than he'd hoped.

"I came to see you."

"Just passing through, I guess." She was thinner than she'd been when he left. What had he done to her? It made him heart sick.

"A little more than that."

She patted PG's nose. "I thought you'd be off in India or someplace by now."

Callee wasn't giving him an inch. What had he expected, a warm welcome? He'd hurt her. It was time for some fast talking. "Can we talk?"

"I'm busy here." She picked up the brush. "I thought we said all there was to say before you left."

"Yeah, but I've accepted something while I was gone that has changed things."

"And that would be?" She started brushing PG once more.

He stepped closer. "Callee, do you think you could look at me?"

"No."

The word was so soft he almost missed it. "Why not?"

"Because it's too hard." There was a catch in her voice.

Was she crying? His chest tightened.

"Why'd you come back here anyway? You said to cut it off so it wouldn't hurt."

"I'm trying to tell you why I'm here."

She spun around and glared at him. "Then tell me."

"Because I love you."

Callee blinked. Her eyes brightened and a smile flashed across her face. She dropped the brush and started toward him. He opened his arms and she jumped into them, wrapping her arms around his neck and holding him tight.

Her mouth found his in a smacking kiss that rocked his world. Callee was his world.

"I love you too." She kissed his eyes, his cheek, his temple and nibbled at his ear.

He kissed her long and tenderly with all the love in his heart. Finally, he let her slip along his body until her feet touched the sawdust floor.

"Wait here." She took PG to a stall and closed him in.

"Callee, we still need to talk."

"I have something I want to tell you too." She took his hand. "Come with me." She led him outside to a bench resting against the side of the barn. They sat.

Langston twisted until he faced her. He pulled a piece of hay out of her hair. "Do you think the Thompsons are wondering what we are doing?"

"They're off hunting a new house." She kissed him. "They'll be gone all afternoon. May I talk first?"

"You keep that up and you can have anything you want." He returned a kiss.

She held him back when he would have gone further. "I want to tell you my news."

"That is?"

"I talked to my father." She beamed. "He said he was proud of me. All is good between us. I should have told him how I felt sooner."

"That's wonderful. I know that makes you very happy."

Callee sat straighter, with her shoulders back. "I'm going to resign from the clinic. I'm going to take that job with Dr. Mitchell."

"So you decided to do that. That's wonderful. I think it's tailor-made for you."

"I believe it is too. I never would have considered it if it hadn't been for you and what you said. You were right. I have been hiding and paying my guilt penitence for Joe. You made me see that. Thank you." She gave him a quick kiss. "The best part is I'll have the freedom to travel with you or visit you or however you want to work this out between us. All I know is I want you in my life."

"About that…"

Callee's heart lodged in her throat. She dared not guess what he would say next. Fearing he wouldn't want her traveling with him or worse not to even try long distance.

"I'm coming to Louisville to start a Valtech office here. I'll still be doing research but in affiliation with the university. I'm also going to be on the staff at the hospital. There'll still be some travel but not as much as I've been doing."

"You're moving here?" Callee looked at Langston in disbelief. Was her dream really coming true? She shook her head. "No, I can't let you do that for me. You'll hate it, then you'll start resenting me. I want you to be happy."

"Sweetheart," he said, kissing her quiet. "I'll be happy anywhere you are."

She cupped his whisker-roughened cheeks and kissed him like he was the most wonderful man she knew, and he was. She pulled away. "Are you sure?"

"I'm sure. You aren't the only one who listened to some truths. I thought about what you said to me too. I went to Prairie. Visited Mark and Emily."

Callee's mouth formed an O. "That must have been hard for you."

"It was but therapeutic as well. I think I was hurt on two fronts. By Emily, but also by losing my best friend as well. I hope we'll find our way back to some of what we had. They want to meet you."

"You told them about me?"

"I sure did." He brushed her hair away from her face. "Emily knew right away I was in love."

"Did you see your parents?" She hoped it went well.

"I did. It was nice. I've hurt them, but they love

me so they'll give me a chance to do better. They helped me come up with my plan."

"Your plan for what?"

"For my new jobs, coming here to see you and one more thing."

"I still don't understand." Callee remained completely confused.

"I'm sorry. I think I'm going about this a little backward. I love you and I want you in my life forever." He scooted off the bench and went to one knee, taking her left hand. "I'm totally under your spell, Callee Dobson. Yours forever."

Callee's heart fluttered. This couldn't be... She'd dreamed it but never imagined Langston would...

"Will you marry me?"

"Yes. A thousand times yes." She launched herself at him making him fall to the ground. He grabbed her around the waist and held her tight. She kissed him with all the love in her heart. Minutes later her legs straddled his hips as she looked into his beautiful eyes, which returned her admiration and love. "I love you so much, Langston. I want you to be happy."

"I am when I'm with you."

A few minutes later she helped Langston up and they dusted themselves off. "Well, I was thinking that if I was going to have a wife—" he smiled at her "—that we should have a place where we could raise our children and keep her horse. Maybe some place like this, if she liked it."

Callee looked at him in disbelief. "You're not thinking of buying the farm, are you?"

He shrugged. "Only if it is what you want."

Her eyes widened. "I can't believe it. You would really want to live here?"

"If it would make you happy, it would make me happy."

Callee smiled. "It sounds perfect to me. You know I love this farm, but the most important thing is you'll be living here with me. All I've ever really wanted is your cowboy boots beside my bed—forever."

"Honey, this man is finished wandering. I've found my home. You."

* * * * *

Look out for the next story in the
Kentucky Derby Medics duet!

And if you enjoyed this story, check out these
other great reads from Susan Carlisle

Second Chance for the Heart Doctor
Wedding Date with Her Best Friend
Reunited with the Children's Doc
Mending the ER Doc's Heart

All available now!